THE LEWIS CARROLL PUZZLE BOOK

'My name is Alice, but—'
'It's a stupid enough name!' Humpty Dumpty interrupted impatiently.
'What does it mean?'
'Must a name mean something?' Alice asked doubtfully.

THE LEWIS CARROLL PUZZLE BOOK

A COLLECTION OF CLASSIC CONUNDRUMS

INTRODUCTION AND AFTERWORD BY BRIAN SIBLEY
COMPILED BY EMMA MARRIOTT

PEGASUS BOOKS
NEW YORK LONDON

THE LEWIS CARROLL PUZZLE BOOK

Pegasus Books, Ltd.
148 West 37th Street, 13th Floor
New York, NY 10018

First Pegasus Books cloth edition June 2025

ISBN: 978-1-63936-905-8

10 9 8 7 6 5 4 3 2 1

Printed in the United States of America
Distributed by Simon & Schuster
www.pegasusbooks.com

CONTENTS

INTRODUCTION

by Brian Sibley

'Oh dear, how puzzling it all is!'

Alice's adventures in Wonderland and her later exploits in the looking-glass world frequently leave her 'puzzled', a word that – along with 'puzzling' – is repeatedly used by Lewis Carroll to describe his heroine's state of mind. That is hardly surprising since the stories are full of questions and questions are invariably puzzles in search of solutions.

Alice is constantly being asked questions: 'Who are *you*?', 'What's your name, child?', 'How old did you say you were?', 'Where do you come from? . . . And where are you going?' Alice also asks a great many questions of the characters she meets: 'Please would you tell me . . . why your cat grins like that?', 'Which way ought I to go from here?', 'Why did they live at the bottom of a well?' and 'Why are you painting those roses?'

Indeed, she even asks herself questions, from her falling-down-the-rabbit-hole pondering – 'Do cats eat bats? . . . Do bats eat cats?' – to perhaps her most searching speculation: 'Who in the world am I? Ah, *that's* the great

Charles Lutwidge Dodgson ('Lewis Carroll') aged 43. An 'assisted self-portrait', photographed in May 1875 in his Rooftop Studio in Tom Quad, Christ Church, Oxford.

puzzle!', a philosophical proposition worthy of Shakespeare's Prince of Denmark.

Which brings us to more prosaic questions regarding the present volume: what is it and what is it not? This book – which, incidentally, fulfils Alice's exacting criteria that the only *useful* book is one with pictures and conversations – is a selection of Lewis Carroll's puzzles, problems and pastimes. It includes word-playing games, mathematical conundrums, extracts from Carroll's books and a host of riddles and puzzles that the author set his family and friends throughout his life. It is *not* a comprehensive collection of *every* problem posed by Lewis Carroll in his stories, poems, letters and diaries, which would require several volumes far larger and longer than this one. However, this book does provide an intriguing insight into the remarkable, labyrinthine mind of Lewis Carroll as well as a guide to further reading for anyone keen to delve further into Carrollian bemusements.

Confronted on the doorstep of the Duchess's house by the less than helpful Frog Footman, Alice asks, 'How am I to get in?' The Footman's frustrating response is, 'Are you to get in at all? . . . That's the first question, you know.'

The first question with which, perhaps, *we* ought to have begun is: why did Lewis Carroll indulge in quite so much puzzle-posing? The answer, if it's not too late – and 'Oh my ears and whiskers, how late it's getting!' – is that it began long before he ever *became* 'Lewis Carroll'.

Meet Charles Lutwidge Dodgson (the 'g' in 'Dodgson', by the way, is silent): he was born on 27 January 1832 at All Saints' Vicarage in Daresbury, a rural village in Cheshire, where his father was a Church of England priest. Young Charles was the third oldest and first-born boy of eleven children.

In 1843, when Charles was eleven, his father was appointed Rector of the

Church of St Peter in the North Yorkshire village of Croft-on-Tees. The boy was soon a central player in the busy life of the happy and creative family in Croft Rectory: impresario (playwright, actor and director) of the toy theatre; juvenile conjuror; and editor of a series of family magazines, with such titles as *Useful and Instructive Poetry*, *The Rectory Magazine* and *Mischmasch*: home-made projects featuring stories, verses, elaborate illustrations and topical cartoons, the majority of which were his own invention. Additionally, he devised numerous games and diversions with which to entertain his adoring siblings, some of which are featured in this book. These childhood pleasures were but the beginning of what would prove a lifetime's preoccupation with puzzling propositions.

An illustration by the young Charles Dodgson from *The Rectory Umbrella*, compiled between 1850–1853, one of several domestic magazines made 'for the amusement of his brothers and sisters'.

After home-schooling, Charles was educated at Richmond Grammar School and Rugby where, although unhappy with the public-school environment, he excelled in mathematics. His already established love of words, his growing fascination with numbers and logical thinking began to meld into a unique approach to the perplexing, but inevitable, collision of mathematical certainties and linguistic flexibilities. From these tussles grew the brilliant word-and-number-play that would be such a vibrant part of his creative writing.

In 1850, Charles, like his father before him, was accepted by Christ Church, Oxford, which would remain his home for the rest of his life. He gained his Bachelor of Arts degree in 1854 and, the following year, was appointed Mathematical Lecturer. Prior to taking up this role, he gained teaching practice at the local Church of England School established by his father in Croft. More experience was gained at St Aldgate's School, Oxford, where he handled rumbunctious classes by peppering his tutorials with established number-puzzles to engage and entertain his pupils while introducing serious mathematical concepts. You'll find a trio of such playful challenges in the pages that follow. In 1861, Charles was ordained a Deacon of the Church of England but, whilst he used the title 'Reverend', he did not proceed to priesthood.

He continued writing verse and, in 1856, first used his famous *nom de plume* when publishing a poem in the magazine, *The Train*. Dodgson had offered the editor a selection of pseudonyms including 'Edgar Cuthwellis', 'Edgar U. C. Westhill' (both anagrams of 'Charles Lutwidge') and 'Lewis Carroll', which he had devised by translating his first and middle names into Latin – *Carolus Ludovicus* – and then reversing and anglicising them into Lewis Carroll. The editor earned his place in history by choosing the latter.

The same year, Charles took up the popular Victorian pastime of photography, proving a fine portraitist and one of the leading amateur photographers

A coloured version of John Tenniel's frontispiece illustration to *Alice's Adventures in Wonderland.*

of the age. The camera proved a useful entrée to Oxford society and to a wider cultural circle including such notables as John Ruskin, Dante Gabriel Rossetti and the nation's Poet Laureate, Alfred, Lord Tennyson. His skill as a photographer also led to a friendship with the children of Dr. Henry George Liddell, the Dean of Christ Church.

It was during a boat trip on the Thames on 4 July 1862 with three of the Liddell children – Lorina, Alice and Edith – that he extemporised a fanciful tale of 'another Alice' and her adventures in a curious subterranean world. At the behest of the character's namesake, Dodgson wrote out and illustrated the story calling it *Alice's Adventures Under Ground*.

Encouraged by friends, Dodgson – let's call him Carroll from now on – expanded the story (adding a Duchess, a Cheshire Cat and a Mad Tea-Party), engaged the celebrated illustrator, John Tenniel and, in 1865, published the result as *Alice's Adventures in Wonderland*. The book's freedom of invention and lack of didacticism would prove a milestone in the development of children's fiction.

A publication success, *Wonderland* was followed, in 1871, by a sequel, *Through the Looking-Glass and What Alice Found There* and, five years later, an epic nonsense ballad, *The Hunting of the Snark*: books filled with more mathematical and logical conundrums, puzzling – and sometimes alarming – dilemmas about dreams, portents, names and identities and issues concerning the importance of rules and the observation of rituals.

Carroll also wrote several books of verse and *Sylvie and Bruno*, a two-part fantasy novel (1889 and 1893), now largely unappreciated but, nevertheless, a rich repository of overlooked nonsense.

In addition to Carroll's serious mathematical writings – begun in 1860 with *A Syllabus of Plane Algebraical Geometry* – he used his reputation as a storyteller to publish books of mathematical and logical games and puzzles such as *Doublets, A Word Puzzle* (1879), *A Tangled Tale* (1885), *The Game of Logic* (1886), and *Symbolic Logic* (1896). In 1891, being a lover of gadgets and borderline insomniac, Carroll addressed the problem of recording night-time thoughts with the invention of the 'nyctograph', a device for making notes in the dark. Four years later, he published *Pillow-Problems Thought Out During Sleepless Nights* as a distraction for fellow restless sleepers. You will find some examples in this book.

Lewis Carroll's fertile imagination constantly buzzed and fizzed with possibilities and propositions: inventing new board games; composing acrostic poems in which the names of friends were hidden in plain sight; filling his letters with visual and verbal riddles, mazes and pictographs. He offered 'Wise Words' for better letter-writing; devised a means for finding the day of the week for any date (see page 80) and proposed alternative systems for parliamentary representation and amendments to the rules in tennis tournaments. He even came up with his own variation on the Queen of Hearts' favourite recreation, croquet!

Lewis Carroll lived a full life, associating with noted scholars and clerics, significant figures in art, literature and the world of theatre and making many friends, young and old. He died at Guildford on 14 January 1898, leaving a rare and memorable legacy of poetic sense and 'nonsensesibility' that is beloved by the world and shows no sign of ever being contrariwise.

So, now you know all you need to know to start tackling the brainteasers that follow but, like Alice, be prepared to be 'thoroughly puzzled'!

OPPOSITE: The combined talents of Lewis Carroll the storyteller and illustrator John Tenniel resulted in the creation of an immortal classic of world literature.

The
MACMILLAN
ALICE
The
MACMILLAN
ALICE

PUZZLES

The
MACMILLAN
ALICE

Down the Rabbit-Hole

EXCERPT FROM *Alice's Adventures in Wonderland*, Chapter 1

At the beginning of *Alice's Adventures in Wonderland* Alice spots a White Rabbit with a pocket-watch and follows him as he disappears down a large rabbit-hole. She begins to fall and as she does, she looks around and considers what might happen next.

Down, down, down. Would the fall never *come to an end? 'I wonder how many miles I've fallen by this time?' she said aloud. 'I must be getting somewhere near the centre of the earth. Let me see: that would be four thousand miles down, I think—' (for, you see, Alice had learnt several things of this sort in her lessons in the schoolroom, and though this was not a very good opportunity for showing off her knowledge, as there was no one to listen to her, still it was good practice to say it over) '—yes, that's about the right distance – but then I wonder what Latitude or Longitude I've got to?' (Alice had no idea what Latitude was, or Longitude either, but thought they were nice grand words to say.)*

Presently she began again. 'I wonder if I shall fall right through *the earth!'*

What would happen to Alice if the hole went straight through the centre of the earth? How far is the centre of the earth from the surface of Alice's garden?

Drink Me

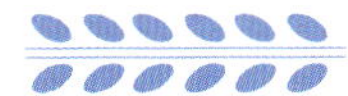

EXCERPT FROM *Alice's Adventures in Wonderland*, Chapter 1

There seemed to be no use in waiting by the little door, so she went back to the table, half hoping she might find another key on it, or at any rate a book of rules for shutting people up like telescopes: this time she found a little bottle on it ('which certainly was not here before,' said Alice,) and round the neck of the bottle was a paper label, with the words 'DRINK ME' beautifully printed on it in large letters.

Alice goes on to drink from the bottle and discovers it has a tasty mix of flavours. A contemporary of Lewis Carroll remembers how the author liked to 'quiz' his neighbours at the dinner table 'with occasional conundrums with a mathematical air'. Here is one of his drink-related puzzles.

Take two tumblers, one of which contains 50 spoonfuls of pure brandy and the other 50 spoonfuls of pure water. Take from the first of these one spoonful of the brandy and transfer it without spilling into the second tumbler and stir it up. Then take a spoonful of the mixture and transfer it back without spilling to the first tumbler.

If you consider the whole transaction, has more brandy been transferred from the first tumbler to the second, or more water from the second tumbler to the first?

A Boating Trip

Lewis Carroll was a master of the acrostic poem, hiding the names of friends in plain sight as he does in this poem which appears at the end of *Through the Looking-Glass*. It recalls a boating trip he made in 1862 when he first told the story of *Alice's Adventures in Wonderland*. Can you find the name concealed in the poem?

A BOAT, beneath a sunny sky,
Lingering onward dreamily
In an evening of July –

Children three that nestle near,
Eager eye and willing ear,
Pleased a simple tale to hear –

Long has paled that sunny sky;
Echoes fade and memories die;
Autumn frosts have slain July.

Still she haunts me, phantomwise,
Alice moving under skies
Never seen by waking eyes.

Children yet, the tale to hear,
Eager eye and willing ear,
Lovingly shall nestle near.

In a Wonderland they lie,
Dreaming as the days go by,
Dreaming as the summers die;

Ever drifting down the stream –
Lingering in the golden gleam –
Life, what is it but a dream?

(opposite) * A memorial plaque to Carroll in Poet's Corner in Westminster Abbey, unveiled in 1982, during the 150th anniversary of his birth, carries the inscription: 'Charles Lutwidge Dodgson 1832–98. LEWIS CARROLL. Student of Christ Church Oxford. Buried at Guildford. "Is all our Life, then, but a dream?"'

But a Dream?

An acrostic poem appears in the preface to *Sylvie and Bruno*, a novel by Lewis Carroll first published in 1889. It poses a similar philosophical question to the acrostic opposite published seventeen years earlier. It is dedicated to another friend of Carroll and her name is hidden twice in this 'double acrostic'. Can you decipher the name and see where it is hidden?

Is all our Life, then, but a dream*
Seen faintly in the golden gleam
Athwart Time's dare resistless
  stream?

Bowed to the earth with bitter woe,
Or laughing at some raree-show,
We flutter idly to and fro.

Man's little Day in haste we spend,
And, from its merry noontide, send
No glance to meet the silent end.

How Puzzling!

EXCERPT FROM *Alice's Adventures in Wonderland*, Chapter 2

Lots of strange things have been happening to Alice and she wonders whether she's been changed into another girl in the night and now she can't remember her multiplication tables.

Alice took up the fan and gloves, and, as the hall was very hot, she kept fanning herself all the time she went on talking: 'Dear, dear! How queer everything is today! And yesterday things went on just as usual. I wonder if I've been changed in the night? Let me think: was *I the same when I got up this morning? I almost think I can remember feeling a little different. But if I'm not the same, the next question is, Who in the world am I? Ah,* that's *the great puzzle!' And she began thinking over all the children she knew that were of the same age as herself, to see if she could have been changed for any of them.*

'I'm sure I'm not Ada,' she said, 'for her hair goes in such long ringlets, and mine doesn't go in ringlets at all; and I'm sure I can't be Mabel, for I know all sorts of things, and she, oh! she knows such a very little! Besides, she's *she, and*

I'm *I, and – oh dear, how puzzling it all is! I'll try if I know all the things I used to know. Let me see: four times five is twelve, and four times six is thirteen, and four times seven is – oh dear! I shall never get to twenty at that rate!'*

Why will Alice never get to twenty?

The Mouse's Tale

The words of the poem 'The Mouse's Tale' is shaped to mimic the tail of a mouse, a play on the homonyms 'tale' and 'tail'. Lewis Carroll's original handwritten version of the story *Alice's Adventures Under Ground* contained a different verse in which the mouse explains why he hates cats and dogs.

We lived beneath the mat
Warm and snug and fat
But one woe, & that
Was the cat!
To our joys
a clog, In
our eyes a
fog, On our
hearts a log
Was the dog!
When the
cat's away,
Then
the mice
will
play,
But, alas!
one day, (So they say)
Came the dog and
cat, Hunting
for a
rat,
Crushed
the mice
all flat,
Each
one
as
he
sat
Underneath the mat,
Warm 'n' snug, & fat –
Think of that!

"Fury said to
a mouse, That
he met in the
house, 'Let
us both go
to law: *I*
will prose-
cute *you*.—
Come, I'll
take no de-
nial: We
must have
the trial;
For really
this morn-
ing I've
nothing
to do.'
Said the
mouse to
the cur,
'Such a
trial, dear
sir, With
no jury
or judge,
would
be wast-
ing our
breath.'
'I'll be
judge,
I'll be
jury,'
said
cun-
ning
old
Fury:
'I'll
try
the
whole
cause,
and
con-
demn
you to
death'."

Cat and Rats

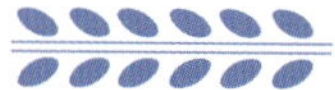

A problem about cats and rats devised by Lewis Carroll appeared in a magazine called *The Monthly Packet* in 1880.

If 6 cats kill 6 rats in 6 minutes, how many will be needed to kill 100 rats in 50 minutes?

According to Carroll there are at least four possible solutions. Can you find four different ways the cats might kill the rats and how many rats will be killed in each instance?

A Fox, a Goose and a Bag of Corn

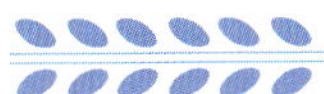

River-crossing puzzles have been popular for centuries and this version involving a man transporting a fox, a goose and a bag of corn was one of the best known. Lewis Carroll described it in a letter to a young friend.

He had to get them over a river, and the boat was so tiny that he could only take *one* across at a time; and he couldn't ever leave the fox and the goose together, for then the fox would eat the goose; and if he left the goose and the corn together, the goose would eat the corn. So the only things he *could* leave safely together were the fox and the corn, for you never see a fox eating corn; and you hardly ever see corn eating a fox.

How did he do it?

Where Does the Day Begin?

EXCERPT FROM *Alice's Adventures in Wonderland*, Chapter 6

'If everybody minded their own business,' the Duchess said in a hoarse growl, 'the world would go round a deal faster than it does.'

'Which would not *be an advantage,' said Alice, who felt very glad to get an opportunity of showing off a little of her knowledge. 'Just think what work it would make with the day and night! You see the earth takes twenty-four hours to turn round on its axis—'*

'Talking of axes,' said the Duchess, 'chop off her head!'

Alice glanced rather anxiously at the cook, to see if she meant to take the hint; but the cook was busily stirring the soup, and seemed not to be listening, so she went on again: 'Twenty-four hours, I think; *or is it twelve? I—'*

'Oh, don't bother me,*' said the Duchess. 'I never could abide figures!'*

Questions concerning the rotation of the earth and the working of time perplexed Lewis Carroll throughout much of his life. As a teenager sometime in 1849 or 1850, he posed the following to his brothers and sisters in his family magazine *The Rectory Umbrella*.

∴

Half of the world, or nearly so, is always in the light of the sun: as the world turns round, this hemisphere of light shifts round too, and passes over each part of it in succession.

Supposing on Tuesday, it is morning in London; in another hour it would be Tuesday morning in the west of England; if the whole world were land we might go on tracing* Tuesday morning, Tuesday morning all the way round, till in 24 hours we get to London again. But we *know* that at London 24 hours after Tuesday morning it is Wednesday morning. Where then, in its passage round the earth, does the day change its name? Where does it lose its identity?

What is the solution?

* The best way is to imagine yourself walking round with the sun and asking the inhabitants as you go 'What morning is this?' If you suppose them living all the way round, and all speaking one language, the difficulty is obvious.

Anagrams

Lewis Carroll's love of word games included devising and working out anagrams. Some that he created for well-known people of the day followed the nineteenth-century fashion for making the anagram descriptive of its subject.

Here are two of Carroll's anagrams for well-known names in the Victorian era; one became a British prime minister in 1868 and the other came to prominence during the Crimean War. Can you work out the names?

Wild agitator! Means well.*

Flit on, cheering angel.

* Lewis Carroll also invented two other anagrams for this name: 'A wild man will go at trees' and 'Wilt tear down all images?'

Mischmasch

Lewis Carroll delighted in inventing games of all types including the word game Mischmasch. The goal is to find as many words as possible that contain a set of two of more letters, called a 'nucleus'. This version of the rules and scoring system was printed in 1886.

A WORD GAME FOR TWO PLAYERS
OR TWO SETS OF PLAYERS

THE essence of this game consists in one Player proposing a "nucleus" (i.e. a set of two or more letters, such as "gp," "emo," "imse"), and in the other trying to find a "lawful word" (i.e. a word known in ordinary society, and not a proper name), containing it. Thus, "magpie," "lemon," "himself," are lawful words containing the nuclei "gp," "emo," "imse".

A nucleus must not contain a hyphen (e.g. for the nucleus "erga," "flower-garden" is not a lawful word).

Any word, that is always printed with a capital initial (e.g. "English"), counts as a proper name.

1. Each thinks of a nucleus, and says "ready" when he has done so. When both have spoken, the nuclei are named. A Player may set a nucleus without knowing of any word containing it.
2. When a Player has guessed a word containing the nucleus set to him (which need not be the word thought of by the Player who set it), or has made up his mind that there is no such word, or that there is one, but he cannot guess it, he says "ready." When he has decided to give up trying, he says "I resign". The other must then, within a stated time (e.g. 2 minutes), say "ready," or "not ready". If he says nothing, he is assumed to be "not ready."
3. When both have spoken, if the first speaker has guessed a word, he names the word he has guessed: if he says "no word," he who set the nucleus, names, if he can, a word containing it. The other Player then proceeds in the same way.
4. The Players then score as follows : — (N.B. — When a Player is said to "lose" marks, it means that the other scores them.)

Guessing a word,	rightly,	scores 2.
" "	wrongly,	loses 2.
Guessing "no word,"	rightly,	scores 3.
" "	wrongly,	loses 3.
Resigning,		loses 1.

This ends the first move.

5. For every other move, the Players proceed as for the first move, except that when a Player is "not ready," or has guessed a word wrongly, he has not a new nucleus set to him, but goes on guessing the one already in hand, having first, if necessary, set a new nucleus for the other Player.
6. A "resigned" nucleus cannot be set again during the same game.
7. The move, in which either scores 10, is the final one; when it is completed, the game is over, and the highest score wins, or, if the scores be equal, the game is drawn.

The Cheshire Cat

EXCERPT FROM *Alice's Adventures in Wonderland*, Chapter 6

The Cat only grinned when it saw Alice. It looked good natured, she thought: still it had *very* long claws and a great many teeth, so she felt that it ought to be treated with respect.

'Cheshire Puss,' she began, rather timidly, as she did not at all know whether it would like the name: however, it only grinned a little wider. 'Come, it's pleased so far,' thought Alice, and she went on. 'Would you tell me, please, which way I ought to go from here?'

'That depends a good deal on where you want to get to,' said the Cat.

'I don't much care where—' said Alice.

'Then it doesn't matter which way you go,' said the Cat.

'—so long as I get *somewhere*,' Alice added as an explanation.

'Oh, you're sure to do that,' said the Cat, 'if you only walk long enough.'

Alice felt that this could not be denied, so she tried another question. 'What sort of people live about here?'

'In *that* direction,' the Cat said, waving its right paw round, 'lives a Hatter: and in *that* direction,' waving the other paw, 'lives a March Hare. Visit either you like: they're both mad.'

'But I don't want to go among mad people,' Alice remarked.

'Oh, you can't help that,' said the Cat:

'we're all mad here. I'm mad. You're mad.'

'How do you know I'm mad?' said Alice.

'You must be,' said the Cat, 'or you wouldn't have come here.'

Alice didn't think that proved it at all; however, she went on: 'And how do you know that you're mad?'

'To begin with,' said the Cat, 'a dog's not mad. You grant that?'

'I suppose so,' said Alice.

'Well, then,' the Cat went on, 'you see, a dog growls when it's angry, and wags its tail when it's pleased. Now I growl when I'm pleased, and wag my tail when I'm angry. Therefore I'm mad.'

'*I* call it purring, not growling,' said Alice.

'Call it what you like,' said the Cat. 'Do you play croquet with the Queen today?'

'I should like it very much,' said Alice, 'but I haven't been invited yet.'

'You'll see me there,' said the Cat, and vanished.

Alice was not much surprised at this, she was getting so used to queer things happening. While she was looking at the place where it had been, it suddenly appeared again.

'By the by, what became of the baby?' said the Cat. 'I'd nearly forgotten to ask.'

'It turned into a pig,' Alice answered very quietly, just as if it had come back in a natural way.

'I thought it would,' said the Cat, and vanished again.

Alice waited a little, half expecting to see it again, but it did not appear, and after a minute or two she walked on in the direction in which the March Hare was said to live. 'I've seen hatters before,' she said to herself; 'the March Hare will be much the most interesting, and perhaps as this is May it won't be raving mad – at least not so mad as it was in March.' As she said this, she looked up, and there was the Cat again, sitting on a branch of a tree.

'Did you say pig, or fig?' said the Cat.

'I said pig,' replied Alice; 'and I wish you wouldn't keep appearing and vanishing so suddenly: you make one quite giddy.'

Stop the Clocks

EXCERPT FROM *Alice's Adventures in Wonderland*, Chapter 7

Alice had been looking over his shoulder with some curiosity. 'What a funny watch!' she remarked. 'It tells the day of the month, and doesn't tell what o'clock it is!'

'Why should it?' muttered the Hatter. 'Does your *watch tell you what year it is?'*

'Of course not,' Alice replied very readily: 'but that's because it stays the same year for such a long time together.'

'Which is just the case with mine*,' said the Hatter.*

Alice felt dreadfully puzzled. The Hatter's remark seemed to her to have no sort of meaning in it, and yet it was certainly English. 'I don't quite understand you,' she said, as politely as she could.

In *Alice's Adventures in Wonderland* the Hatter's watch gives only the date, not hours or minutes, which is perhaps not surprising as time has been frozen in his world. In fact, we are told the Hatter has fallen out with 'Time' and is now trapped in a space devoid of it. Consequently, it is always six o'clock at his tea-party. The capricious nature of time had long fascinated Lewis Carroll and as a young man he posed two puzzles under the title of 'Difficulties' around the theme of stopped clocks in his family magazine, *The Rectory Umbrella*. See if you can answer them.

1. Which is the best, a clock that is right only once a year, or a clock that is right twice every day?

2. I have two clocks: one doesn't go *at all*, and the other loses a minute a day: which would you prefer?

The Mock Turtle's Story

EXCERPT FROM *Alice's Adventures in Wonderland*, Chapter 9

'I only took the regular course.'

'What was that?' enquired Alice.

'Reeling and Writhing, of course, to begin with,' the Mock Turtle replied; 'and then the different branches of Arithmetic – Ambition, Distraction, Uglification, and Derision.'

'I never heard of "Uglification",' Alice ventured to say. 'What is it?'

The Gryphon lifted up both its paws in surprise. 'What! Never heard of uglifying!' it exclaimed. 'You know what to beautify is, I suppose?'

'Yes,' said Alice doubtfully: 'it means – to – make – anything – prettier.'

'Well, then,' the Gryphon went on, 'if you don't know what to uglify is, you are *a simpleton.'*

Alice did not feel encouraged to ask any more questions about it, so she turned to the Mock Turtle and said, 'What else had you to learn?'

'Well, there was Mystery,' the Mock Turtle replied, counting off the subjects on his flappers, – 'Mystery, ancient and modern, with Seaography: then Drawling – the Drawling-master was an old conger-eel, that used to come once a week. He *taught us Drawling, Stretching, and Fainting in Coils.'*

'What was that like?' said Alice.

'Well, I can't show it you myself,' the Mock Turtle said: 'I'm too stiff. And the Gryphon never learnt it.'

'Hadn't time,' said the Gryphon: 'I went to the Classics master, though. He was an old crab, he *was.'*

'I never went to him,' the Mock Turtle said with a sigh. 'He taught Laughing and Grief, they used to say.'

'So he did, so he did,' said the Gryphon, sighing in his turn; and both creatures hid their faces in their paws.

'And how many hours a day did you do lessons?' said Alice, in a hurry to change the subject.

'Ten hours the first day,' said the Mock Turtle: 'nine the next, and so on.'

'What a curious plan!' exclaimed Alice.

'That's the reason they're called lessons,' the Gryphon remarked: 'because they lessen from day to day.'

This was quite a new idea to Alice, and she thought it over a little before she made her next remark. 'Then the eleventh day must have been a holiday?'

'Of course it was,' said the Mock Turtle.

'And how did you manage on the twelfth?' Alice went on eagerly.

'That's enough about lessons,' the Gryphon interrupted in a very decided tone. 'Tell her something about the games now.'

The Mock Turtle tells Alice about how he went to school in the sea where his master was an old turtle called Tortoise. He explains: 'We called him Tortoise because he taught us . . . '

The curriculum described is, of course, a series of puns on traditional school subjects: reading, writing, addition, multiplication, division, history, geography, the art subjects of drawing, sketching and painting in oils, and the Classical languages of Latin and Greek. When it comes to the curious concept of lessening hours in the school day, Alice eagerly wants to know what happened on the twelfth day, but the Gryphon brings their discussion to an abrupt end, perhaps because the maths has come to an end and there is no answer, or we have entered the realm of disturbing negative numbers to which there is no easy answer.

NUMBER FORTY-TWO

Long before Douglas Adams, author of *The Hitchhiker's Guide to the Galaxy*, famously declared that the number 42 was 'the meaning of life, the universe, and everything', Lewis Carroll was demonstrating a curious fascination with those numerals.

Although 42 is not a particularly significant number in base 13 and whilst Douglas Adams thought of it simply as a joke, for Lewis Carroll it was a mysterious – and *unexplained* – numeric obsession and it repeatedly figures in his writings. Both *Alice's Adventures in Wonderland* and *Through the Looking-Glass* contain 42 illustrations and, now that we have reached an appropriate page in this book, here are a few more examples of Carroll's interesting use of 'Forty-Two'.

From *Alice's Adventures in Wonderland*, Chapter 12 'Alice's Evidence':

> At this moment the King, who had been for some time busily writing in his note-book, cackled out 'Silence!' and read out from his book, 'Rule

Forty-two. *All persons more than a mile high to leave the court.*'

Everybody looked at Alice.

'*I'm* not a mile high,' said Alice.

'You are,' said the King.

'Nearly two miles high,' added the Queen.

'Well, I shan't go, at any rate,' said Alice: 'besides, that's not a regular rule: you invented it just now.'

'It's the oldest rule in the book,' said the King.

'Then it ought to be Number One,' said Alice.

The King turned pale, and shut his note-book hastily. 'Consider your verdict,' he said to the jury, in a low, trembling voice.

∴

In *Through the Looking-Glass*, Chapter 4 'Tweedledum and Tweedledee', these verses appear in the twins' poem about the Walrus and the Carpenter.

The Walrus and the Carpenter
   Were walking close at hand;
They wept like anything to see
   Such quantities of sand:
'If this were only cleared away,'
   They said, 'it would be grand!'

'If seven maids with seven mops
   Swept it for half a year,

Do you suppose,' the Walrus said,
'That they could get it clear?'
'I doubt it,' said the Carpenter,
And shed a bitter tear.

Seven maids working for six months would account for 42 maid-months of labour.

In *Through the Looking-Glass*, Chapter 6 'Humpty Dumpty', Alice is challenged about her age:

> 'So here's a question for you. How old did you say you were?'
> Alice made a short calculation, and said 'Seven years and six months.'
> 'Wrong!' Humpty Dumpty exclaimed triumphantly. 'You never said a word like it!'
> 'I thought you meant 'How old *are* you?'' Alice explained.
> 'If I'd meant that, I'd have said it,' said Humpty Dumpty.
> Alice didn't want to begin another argument, so she said nothing.
> 'Seven years and six months!' Humpty Dumpty repeated thoughtfully. 'An uncomfortable sort of age. Now if you'd asked my advice, I'd have said "Leave off at seven" – but it's too late now.'

Seven years and six months is another sixes-and-sevens combination and, as we know, 7 x 6 = 42.

In *Through the Looking-Glass*, Chapter 7 'The Lion and the Unicorn', the White King tells Alice about all his horses and men in response to Humpty Dumpty's great fall.

> 'I've sent them all!' the King cried in a tone of delight, on seeing Alice. 'Did you happen to meet any soldiers, my dear, as you came through the wood?'

'Yes, I did,' said Alice: 'several thousand, I should think.'

'Four thousand two hundred and seven, that's the exact number,' the King said, referring to his book. 'I couldn't send all the horses, you know, because two of them are wanted in the game.'

Four thousand two hundred and seven can also be written as 4207, and 42 and 07 is a factor of 42.

In another of Lewis Carroll's poems, *Phantasmagoria*, a man who is ghost-haunted complains that, considering his years, the spectre who has visited on him is less than impressive:

'No doubt,' said I, 'they settled who
  Was fittest to be sent
Yet still to choose a brat like you,
To haunt a man of forty-two,
  Was no great compliment!'

∴

Some Carroll admirers have become known for their preoccupation with the number: desperate to be the first to purchase number 42 of any limited-edition publications for their collections. Others have contended that there really was an undisclosed reason for Carroll's repeated use of the number and, in seeking to prove it, have reached for explanations that cannot possibly be anything other than conjecture or coincidence, such as the fact that *Wonderland* was first published in 1865 and would, therefore, come out of copyright in 1907, forty-two years later!

∴

In Carroll's epic nonsense poem *The Hunting of the Snark*, this is how one member of the crew (allegedly a Baker) is described:

> There was one who was famed for the number of things
> He forgot when he entered the ship:
> His umbrella, his watch, all his jewels and rings,
> And the clothes he had bought for the trip.
>
> He had forty-two boxes, all carefully packed,
> With his name painted clearly on each:
> But, since he omitted to mention the fact,
> They were all left behind on the beach.
>
> The loss of his clothes hardly mattered, because
> He had seven coats on when he came,
> With three pair of boots – but the worst of it was,
> He had wholly forgotten his name.

Alongside the 42 boxes (which feature in the Henry Holiday illustration opposite) we are told the Baker arrived on board wearing seven coats and three pairs of boots, which would make a total of six boots and another possible 7 x 6 computation.

Four Gentlemen and Their Wives

This puzzle is a similar, although more complex, version of the Fox, the Goose and the Bag of Corn problem. Lewis Carroll probably didn't invent the puzzle but it was one of his favourites. Here it is in the words of Carroll's nephew and biographer Stuart Dodgson Collingwood.

Four gentlemen and their wives wanted to cross the river in a boat that would not hold more than two at a time.

The conditions were that no gentleman must leave his wife on the bank unless with only women or by herself, and also that someone must bring the boat back.

How did they do it?

Magic Numbers

Lewis Carroll enjoyed entertaining his friends with mathematical curiosities, including the following involving 'magic numbers'.

1. Multiply 142,857 with 2, 3, 4, 5, 6 and 7. What do you notice?

2. Find another magic number by doing the following trick.

   Write down a three-digit number with decreasing digits from left to right (such as 643). Then reverse the digits to create a new number and subtract this number from the original number. With the resulting number, add it to the reverse of itself. What number do you get? Try it with other numbers with decreasing digits and what do you notice?

The Monkey and the Weight

Lewis Carroll was bemused by this problem, describing it as 'a most puzzling puzzle', so much so that it caused serious debate with other contemporary mathematicians. Note Carroll is misspelt in the illustration opposite, which first appeared in the book *Sam Loyd's Cyclopedia of 5000 Puzzles, Tricks and Conundrums with Answers* (1914). Lewis Carroll's nephew Stuart Dodgson Collingwood gave the following description of the puzzle.

A rope is supposed to be hung over a wheel fixed to a roof of a building; at one end of the rope a weight is fixed, which exactly counterbalances a monkey which is hanging on to the other end. Suppose that the monkey begins to climb the rope, what will be the result?

(Note: the rope is weightless and perfectly flexible and the pulley is weightless and frictionless.)

LEWIS
CARROL'S
MONKEY
PUZZLE
10
lbs

DOUBLETS

Lewis Carroll invented the word game Doublets in 1877. Published in *Vanity Fair* magazine between 1879 and 1881, doublets proved to be Carroll's most popular word puzzle and they are still played today and commonly known as 'word ladders'. While Carroll developed a slightly more complex scoring method, the main rules are given in his words:

> 'To solve a Doublet, you must change one letter only, in the first word, making a r*eal* word; then change *one* letter only in this new word, and so on till you get to the second word. The intermediate words are called "Links", and the whole thing a "Chain".'

The aim of the game is to complete a chain in the least number of links. As an example, the word 'head' can be changed into the word 'tail' in the following way:

HEAD
heal
teal
tell
tall
TAIL

See if you can complete the chains for these words in the least number of links.

Drive PIG
into STY

PIG

STY

Change TEARS
into SMILE

TEARS

SMILE

Raise FOUR
to FIVE

FOUR

FIVE

PITCH
TENTS

PITCH

TENTS

Make WHEAT
into BREAD

WHEAT

BREAD

Make HARE
into SOUP

HARE

SOUP

Cover EYE
with LID

EYE

LID

Prove PITY
to be GOOD

PITY

GOOD

Turn POOR
into RICH

POUR
|
RICH

Combine ARMY
and NAVY

ARMY
|
NAVY

Change OAT
to RYE

OAT
|
RYE

Place BEANS
on SHELF

BEANS
|
SHELF

Evolve MAN
from APE

APE
|
MAN

QUELL
a BRAVO

QUELL
|
BRAVO

Run COMB
through HAIR

COMB
|
HAIR

BUY
an ASS

BUY
|
ASS

Get COAL
from MINE

MINE
|
COAL

SHAVE
BEARD

SHAVE
|
BEARD

Make KETTLE
HOLDER

KETTLE
|
HOLDER

Turn BROWN
into BLACK

BROWN
|
BLACK

Get GAS
from OIL

OIL
|
GAS

Find GEM
in ORE

ORE
|
GEM

Turn JOHN
into JACK

JOHN
|
JACK

Mend DOOR
with GLUE

DOOR
|
GLUE

Set ONE
a JOB

ONE
|
JOB

Get TOOTH
DRAWN

TOOTH
|
DRAWN

Make SORRY
HAPPY

SORRY
|
HAPPY

Pour OIL
into SEA

OIL
|
SEA

Send MILLER
to MARKET

MILLER
|
MARKET

Change FEAR
into HOPE

FEAR
|
HOPE

Write ODE
to SUN

ODE
|
SUN

Turn IDEA
into FACT

IDEA
|
FACT

Feed OWL
on JAM

OWL

JAM

Cheer BEAVER
with BRANDY

BEAVER

BRANDY

Make ETHEL
WISER

ETHEL

WISER

Draw TEARS
from GLAND

GLAND

TEARS

Pay DEBTS
that are OWING

DEBTS

OWING

Send JOE
to ANN

JOE

ANN

WEEP
under ELMS

ELMS

WEEP

Change TILES
to SLATE

TILES

SLATE

HOAX
a FOOL

HOAX
|
FOOL

Bring COFFEE
after DINNER

DINNER
|
COFFEE

Connect THUR-
SDAY

THUR
|
SDAY

Stow OARS
in BOAT

OARS
|
BOAT

Pluck ACORN
from STALK

STALK
|
ACORN

Turn LOSS
into GAIN

LOSS
|
GAIN

Unite JACK
with JILL

JACK
|
JILL

Change VEAL
into BEEF

VEAL
|
BEEF

Change NOUN
to VERB

NOUN

VERB

WASH
WELL

WASH

WELL

Bring SHIP
to DOCK

SHIP

DOCK

WITH
SOAP

WITH

SOAP

PLANT
BEANS

PLANT

BEANS

Raise UNIT
to FOUR

UNIT

FOUR

Send MONK
to ROME

MONK

ROME

Show COMET
to GAZER

COMET

GAZER

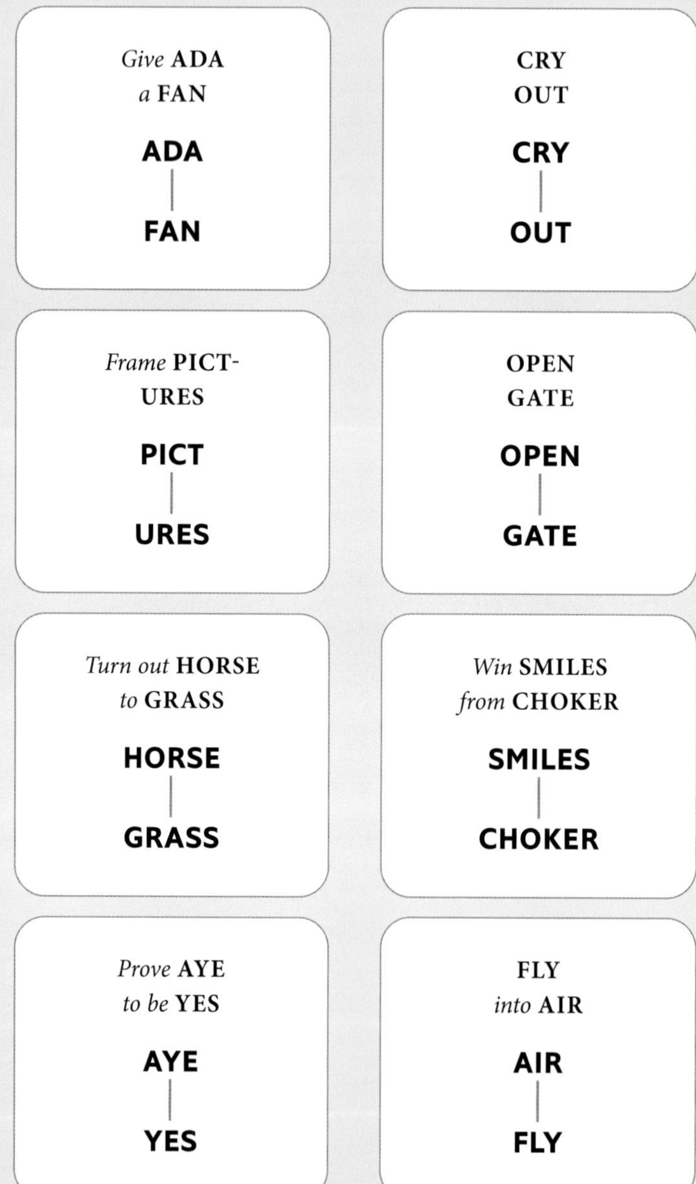

Give ADA
a FAN
ADA
FAN
CRY
OUT
CRY
OUT
Frame PICT-
URES
PICT
URES
OPEN
GATE
OPEN
GATE
Turn out HORSE
to GRASS
HORSE
GRASS
Win SMILES
from CHOKER
SMILES
CHOKER
Prove AYE
to be YES
AYE
YES
FLY
into AIR
AIR
FLY

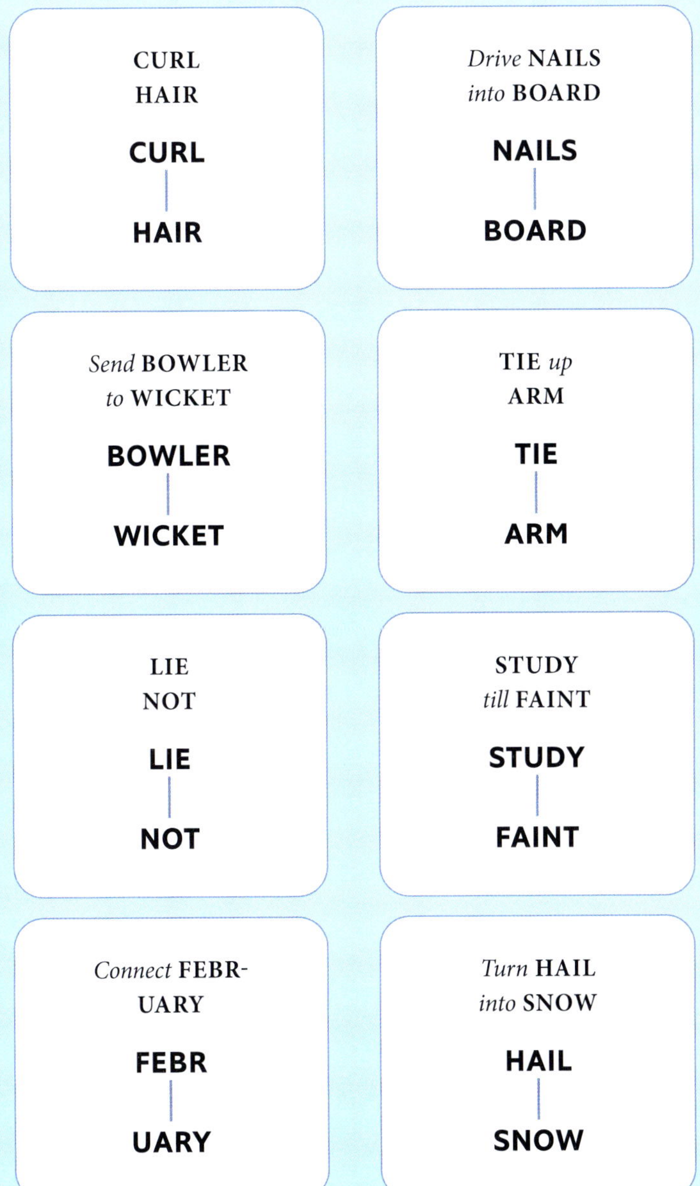
CURL
HAIR
CURL
HAIR
Drive NAILS
into BOARD
NAILS
BOARD
Send BOWLER
to WICKET
BOWLER
WICKET
TIE *up*
ARM
TIE
ARM
LIE
NOT
LIE
NOT
STUDY
till FAINT
STUDY
FAINT
Connect FEBR-
UARY
FEBR
UARY
Turn HAIL
into SNOW
HAIL
SNOW

Put END
to WOE

WOE

|

END

Make CORN
GROW

CORN

|

GROW

HUNT
STAG

HUNT

|

STAG

SHUT
DOOR

SHUT

|

DOOR

BUTTER
LOAVES

BUTTER

|

LOAVES

BEAT
BOYS

BEAT

|

BOYS

Put CRAB
into BOAT

CRAB

|

BOAT

TEACH
GIRLS

TEACH

|

GIRLS

The White Rabbit

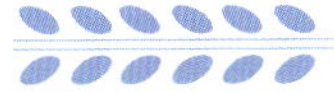

Can you find the White Rabbit in Sir John Tenniel's illustration from *Alice's Adventures in Wonderland*?

Mathematical Tricks

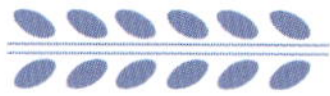

Alongside his lecturing and tutoring at Christ Church, Oxford, Lewis Carroll also tried his hand at school teaching. In 1856 he describes in his diary the various ways he entertained his sometimes boisterous pupils with stories, puzzles and mathematical tricks. He mentioned the name of three tricks outlined below – can you work out how they are done?

THE '9' TRICK

Ask someone to choose any number with a minimum of two digits, then reverse its digits and take away the smaller number from the larger. Once they have an answer ask them to remove any digit other than 0, and then tell you the sum of the remaining digits. You will then be able to tell them which digit they removed.

As an example, they might choose 4618, reverse the digits, to 8164, then subtract the smaller from the larger number, so 8164 – 4618 = 3546. If they remove the number 4, the sum of the remaining numbers is 14. You will then be able to tell them that the number 4 was removed. How do you do it?

THE ADDITION SUM

Ask a person to give you a four-digit number – it could be 2563, and you then write the number 22,561 on a folded piece of paper and put it to one side. You then take it in turns to come up with four more four-digit numbers – the other person comes up with 2146, then you come up with 7853, then the person comes up with 6732, and you come up with 3267. Add the five numbers together and you can reveal that they add up to 22,561, which is the number you wrote on your folded piece of paper. How do you manage that?

COUNTING ALTERNATELY

Start with the number 1, then take it in turns to add any number from 1 to 10. The person that reaches 100 is the winner. As an example, start with 1, the other person adds 5 to make 6, then you add 6 to make 12, then they add 4 to make 16 and you add 7 to make 23, they make 25, you make 34, then 40, 45, 51, 56, 57, 67, 72, 78, 86, 89, 94 and you win because you are the person that gets to 100. How do you make sure you always win?

Lanrick

Lanrick is a board game for two players invented by Lewis Carroll in 1878. An early version of the game, published the following year in 1879, appears below. The game is played on a chess board using chess pawns but the rules are unrelated to chess.

A GAME FOR TWO PLAYERS

The Game is played on a chess-board, each player having 5 men; the other requisites are a die and dice-box, and something (such as a coin) to mark a square.

The interior of the board, excluding the border-squares, is regarded as containing 6 'rows' and 6 'columns.' It must be agreed which is the first row and first column.

1. The players set their men in turn, on any border-squares they like.
2. The die is thrown twice, and a square marked accordingly, the first throw fixing the row, the second the column; the marked square, with the 8 surrounding squares, forms the first 'rendezvous, into which the men are to be played.
3. The men move like chess-queens; in playing for the first 'rendezvous',

each Player may move over 6 squares, either with one man, or dividing the move among several.

4. When one Player has got all his men into the 'rendezvous' the other must remove from the board one of his men that has failed to get in; the die is then thrown for a new 'rendezvous', for which each Player may move over as many squares as he had men in the last 'rendezvous,' and one more.
5. If it be found that either Player has all his men already in the new 'rendezvous,' the die must be thrown again, till a 'rendezvous' is found where this is not the case.
6. The Game ends when one Player has lost all his men.

DUM
DEE

Mirror Image

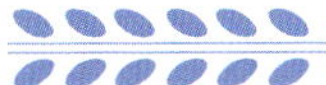

EXCERPT FROM *Through the Looking-Glass*, Chapter 1

'Twas brillig, and the slithy toves
Did gyre and gimble in the wabe;
All mimsy were the borogoves,
And the mome raths outgrabe.

She puzzled over this for some time, but at last a bright thought struck her. 'Why, it's a Looking-Glass book, of course! And if I hold it up to a glass, the words will all go the right way again.'

Lewis Carroll's work is full of references to mirror images, inverted logic and left-right reversals. In the *Alice* books he conveys an upside-down, nonsensical world and in real life Carroll wrote letters in mirror writing or that had to be read from the end word to the first. The strange words in the extract are of course the mirror-image of the first verse of the 'Jabberwocky' poem.

'Twas brillig, and the slithy toves
Did gyre and gimble in the wabe;
All mimsy were the borogoves,
And the mome raths outgrabe.

Can you decipher these well-known phrases from *Alice's Adventures in Wonderland* and *Through the Looking-Glass*?

1. 'Curiouser and curiouser!'

2. 'When I use a word,' Humpty Dumpty said in rather a scornful tone, 'it means just what I choose it to mean – neither more nor less.'

3. 'Off with his head!'

4. 'Why, sometimes I've believed as many as six impossible things before breakfast.'

A Square Window

From his earliest years, Lewis Carroll had been enthused by geometry and many of the puzzles he devised were geometrical in flavour. He posed this problem about a square window letting in too much light in 1873.

A gentleman (a nobleman let us say, to make it more interesting) had a sitting-room with only one window in it – a square window, 3 feet high and 3 feet wide. Now he had weak eyes, and the window gave too much light, so (don't you like "so" in a story?) he sent for the builder, and told him to alter it, so as to give half the light. Only, he was to keep it square – he was to keep it 3 feet high – and he was to keep it 3 feet wide.

How did he do it? Remember, he wasn't allowed to use curtains, or shutters, or coloured glass, or anything of that sort.

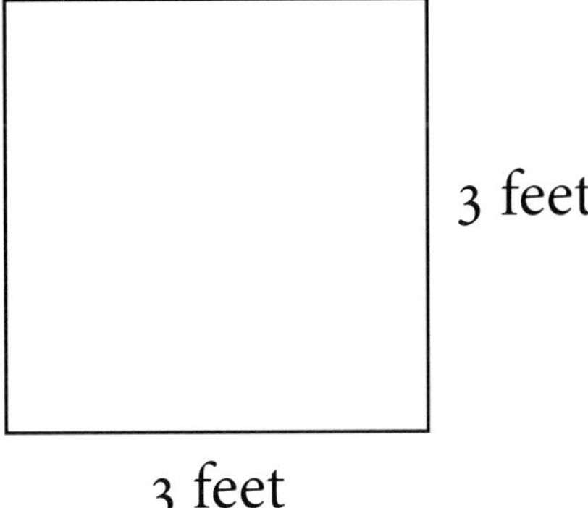

Three Squares

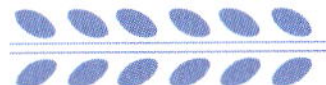

In a letter written in August 1869 Carroll referred to another geometrical puzzle. Can you draw three squares as they are in the diagram below without taking your pencil off the paper or crossing over or repeating any line?

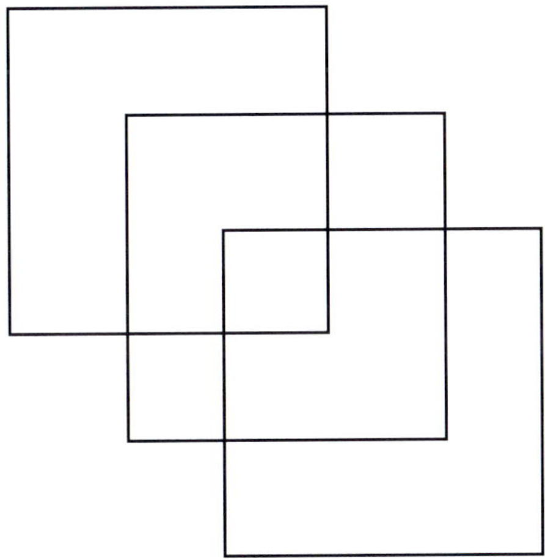

TEA
2/

How to Balance an Egg

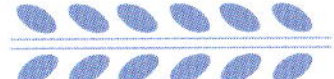

Excerpt from *Through the Looking-Glass*, Chapter 5

The Sheep took the money, and put it away in a box; then she said, 'I never put things into people's hands – that would never do – you must get it for yourself.' And so saying, she went off to the other end of the shop, and set the egg upright on a shelf.

Setting an egg upright on a shelf is a difficult feat.

How can you make an egg stand on its tip?

Days of the Week

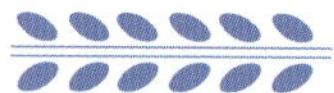

Lewis Carroll came up with a method to calculate the day of the week for any date. He wrote this article for *Nature* magazine in 1887.

Having hit upon the following method of mentally computing the day of the week for any given date, I send it you in the hope that it may interest some of your readers. I am not a rapid computer myself, and as I find my average time for doing any such question is about 20 seconds, I have little doubt that a rapid computer would not need 15.

Take the given date in 4 portions, viz. the number of centuries, the number of years over, the month, the day of the month.

Compute the following 4 items, adding each, whenever found, to the total of the previous items. When an item or total exceeds 7, divide by 7, and keep the remainder only.

The *Century-Item*: For Old Style (which ended September 2, 1752) subtract from 18. The New Style (which began September 14) divide by 4, take over-plus from 3, multiply remainder by 2. [Editor's note: the century-item is the first two digits of the year; e.g., for 1832, take 18.]

The *Year-Item*: Add together the number of dozens, the overplus, and the number of 4's in the overplus.

The *Month-Item*: If it begins or ends with a vowel, subtract the number, denoting its place in the year, from 10. This, plus its number of days, gives the item for the following month. The item for January is "0"; for February or March (the third month), "3"; for December (the 12th month), "12." [Editor's note: in other words, the required numbers, after division by seven, are as follows: January, 0; February, 3; March, 3; April, 6; May, 1; June, 4; July, 6; August, 2; September, 5; October, 0; November, 3; December, 5.]

The *Day-Item*: is the day of the month.

The total, thus reached, must be corrected, by deducting "1" (first adding 7, if the total be "0"), if the date be January or February in a Leap Year: remembering that every year, divisible by 4, is a Leap Year, excepting only the century-years, in New Style, when the number of centuries is *not* so divisible (e.g. 1800).

The final result gives the day of the week, "0" meaning Sunday, "1" meaning Monday, and so on.

EXAMPLES

1783, September 18

17, divided by 4, leaves "1" over; 1 from 3 gives "2"; twice 2 is "4."
83 is 6 dozen and 11, giving 17; plus 2 gives 19, i.e. (dividing by 7) "5."
Total 9, i.e. "2."

The item for August is "8 from 10," i.e. "2"; so, for September, it is "2 plus 3," i.e. "5." Total 7, i.e. "0," which goes out.
18 gives "4." Answer, "*Thursday.*"

1676, February 23

16 from 18 gives "2".
76 is 6 dozen and 4, giving 10; plus 1 gives 11, i.e. "4." Total "6."
The item for February is "3." Total 9, i.e. "2."
23 gives "2." Total "4."
Correction for Leap Year gives "3." Answer, "*Wednesday.*"

Using Carroll's method can you work out the correct days of the week for the following dates?

A. 27 January 1832 – Lewis Carroll is born in Daresbury, Cheshire.

B. 4 July 1862 – on a boating trip in Oxford, Lewis Carroll first tells the story of Alice's Wonderland adventure to Alice Liddell and two of her sisters.

C. 18 November 1865 – first publication of *Alice's Adventures in Wonderland.*

D. 29 March 1876 – first publication of *The Hunting of the Snark.*

E. 14 January 1898 – Lewis Carroll dies in Guildford, Surrey.

Maze

Lewis Carroll drew this complex three-dimensional maze for his younger brothers and sisters in the 1850s. Can you find your way from one of the entrances to the centre?

Running Races

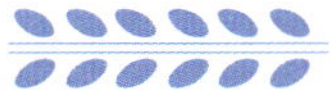

Excerpt from *Through the Looking-Glass*, Chapter 2

'Well, in our *country,' said Alice, still panting a little, 'you'd generally get to somewhere else – if you ran very fast for a long time, as we've been doing.'*

'A slow sort of country!' said the Queen. 'Now, here, *you see, it takes all the running you can do, to keep in the same place. If you want to get somewhere else, you must run at least twice as fast as that!'*

A puzzle based on running a race featured in a letter Lewis Carroll wrote in 1897. It's as follows:

Three men, A, B and C, are to run a race of a quarter-of-a-mile. Whenever A runs against B, he loses 10 yards in every 100; whenever B runs against C, he gains 10 yards in every 100. How should they [runners A and C] be handicapped? ("Handicapping" means that the inferior runners are allowed a start; and the amount is so calculated that, if all were to run at their previous rates, it would be a dead heat: i.e. they would all get to the winning post at the same moment.)

Verse Riddles

Lewis Carroll devised verse riddles for his young friends, seven of which were published in 1870 under the title 'Puzzles from Wonderland'. See if you can answer the first two verse riddles.

1

Dreaming of apples on a wall,
And dreaming often, dear,
I dreamed that if I counted all,
How many would appear?

2

A stick I found, that weighed two pound:
I sawed it up one day
In pieces eight, of equal weight.
How much did each piece weigh?

Humpty Dumpty's Cravat

EXCERPT FROM *Through the Looking-Glass*, Chapter 6

In *Through the Looking Glass*, Alice encounters Humpty Dumpty who is a stickler for the meaning of words but struggles with calculating how many 'un-birthdays' there are in the year.

'It's a cravat, child, and a beautiful one, as you say. It's a present from the White King and Queen. There now!'

'Is it really?' said Alice, quite pleased to find she *had* chosen a good subject, after all.

'They gave it me,' Humpty Dumpty continued thoughtfully, as he crossed one knee over the other and clasped his hands round it, 'they gave it me – for an un-birthday present.'

'I beg your pardon?' Alice said with a puzzled air.

'I'm not offended,' said Humpty Dumpty.

'I mean, what *is* an un-birthday present?'

'A present given when it isn't your birthday, of course.'

Alice considered a little. 'I like birthday presents best,' she said at last.

'You don't know what you're talking about!' cried Humpty Dumpty. 'How many days are there in a year?'

'Three hundred and sixty-five,' said Alice.

'And how many birthdays have you?'

'One.'

'And if you take one from three hundred and sixty-five, what remains?'

'Three hundred and sixty-four, of course.'

Humpty Dumpty looked doubtful. 'I'd rather see that done on paper,' he said.

Alice couldn't help smiling as she took out her memorandum-book, and worked the sum for him:

$$\begin{array}{r} 365 \\ 1 \\ \hline 364 \\ \hline \end{array}$$

Humpty Dumpty took the book, and looked at it very carefully. 'That *seems* to be done right—' he began.

'You're holding it upside down!' Alice interrupted.

'To be sure I was!' Humpty Dumpty said gaily, as she turned it round for him. 'I thought it looked a little queer. As I was saying, that *seems* to be done right – though I haven't time to look it over thoroughly just now – and that shows that there are three hundred and sixty-four days when you might get un-birthday presents—'

'Certainly,' said Alice.

'And only *one* for birthday presents, you know. There's glory for you!'

'I don't know what you mean by "glory",' Alice said.

Humpty Dumpty smiled contemptuously. 'Of course you don't – till I tell you. I meant "there's a nice knockdown argument for you!"'

'But "glory" doesn't mean "a nice knockdown argument",' Alice objected.

'When *I* use a word,' Humpty Dumpty said in rather a scornful tone, 'it means just what I choose it to mean – neither more nor less.'

A Box Riddle

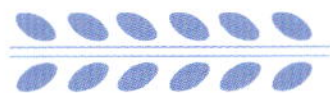

Here is another verse riddle from Lewis Carroll's 'Puzzles from Wonderland'. What kind of box did John give his brother James?

John gave his brother James a box:
About it there were many locks.

James woke, and said it gave him pain;
So gave it back to John again.

This box was not with lid supplied,
Yet caused two lids to open wide:

And all these locks had never a key –
What kind of box, then, could it be?

A Captive Queen

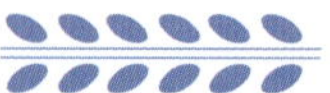

Lewis Carroll's nephew included this problem in a compilation of his uncle's work, *The Lewis Carroll Picture Book* (1899).

A captive Queen and her son and daughter were shut up in the top room of a very high tower. Outside their window was a pulley with a rope round it, and a basket fastened at each end of the rope of equal weight. They managed to escape with the help of this and a weight they found in the room, quite safely. It would have been dangerous for any of them to come down if they weighed more than 15 lbs. more than the contents of the lower basket, for they would do so too quick, and they also managed not to weigh less either.

The one basket coming down would naturally of course draw the other up.

The Queen weighed 195 lbs., daughter 165, son 90, and the weight 75.

How did they do it?

It's My Own Invention

EXCERPT FROM *Through the Looking-Glass*, Chapter 8

The hapless White Knight rescues Alice from the Red Knight but keeps falling off his horse. As an inventor of curious gadgets, it's probable that Lewis Carroll modelled the White Knight on himself. Carroll was equally fond of gadgets and tricks and delighted in coming up with inventions, such as the prototype for travel chess, scrabble and a gum substitute.

She thought she had never seen such a strange-looking soldier in all her life.

He was dressed in tin armour, which seemed to fit him very badly, and he had a queer little deal box fastened across his shoulders, upside-down and with the lid hanging open. Alice looked at it with great curiosity.

'I see you're admiring my little box,' the Knight said in a friendly tone. 'It's my own invention – to keep clothes and sandwiches in. You see I carry it upside-down so that the rain can't get in.'

'But the things can get *out*,' Alice gently remarked. 'Do you know the lid's open?'

'I didn't know it,' the Knight said, a shade of vexation passing over his face.

'Then all the things must have fallen out! And the box is no use without them.' He unfastened it as he spoke, and was just going to throw it into the bushes, when a sudden thought seemed to strike him, and he hung it carefully on a tree. 'Can you guess why I did that?' he said to Alice.

Alice shook her head.

'In hopes some bees may make a nest in it – then I should get the honey.'

'But you've got a beehive – or something like one – fastened to the saddle,' said Alice.

'Yes, it's a very good beehive,' the Knight said in a discontented tone, 'one of the best kind. But not a single bee has come near it yet. And the other thing is a mousetrap. I suppose the mice keep the bees out – or the bees keep the mice out, I don't know which.'

'I was wondering what the mouse-trap was for,' said Alice. 'It isn't very likely there would be any mice on the horse's back.'

'Not very likely, perhaps,' said the Knight; 'but, if they *do* come, I don't choose to have them running all about.'

'You see,' he went on after a pause, 'it's as well to be provided for *everything*. That's the reason the horse has anklets round his feet.'

'But what are they for?' Alice asked in a tone of great curiosity.

'To guard against the bites of sharks,' the Knight replied.

Castle Croquêt

Castle Croquet is a modified version of lawn croquet, which we see Alice playing (using a flamingo for a mallet) in *Alice's Adventures in Wonderland*. Carroll invented the game while he played croquet with the real Alice Liddell and her sisters. This revised version of the game was published in 1866.

FOR FOUR PLAYERS

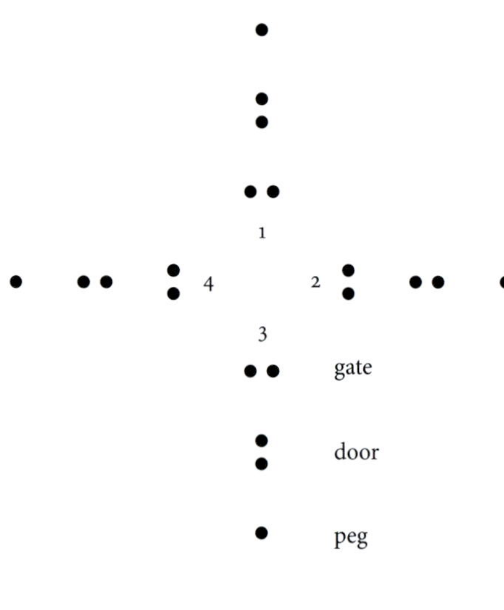

I.

This game requires 8 balls, 8 arches, and 4 pegs:—4 of the balls are called "soldiers;" the others "sentinels." The arches and pegs are set up as in the figure, making 4 "castles," and each player has a castle, a soldier, and a sentinel. Before the game begins, each player places his sentinel within a mallet's length of his peg, and does the same with his soldier when his turn comes to play.

(N.B. The distance from one gate to the next should be 6 or 8 yards, and the distance from the gate to the door, or from the door to the peg, 2 or 3 yards.)

II.

If a sentinel goes through the gate of his castle, in the direction from his peg, he is said to "leave" the castle; when next he goes through it in the opposite direction, he is said to "re-enter" it, and so on. A sentinel, that has not left his castle, is said to be "on duty;" if he leaves it, he is said to be "off duty;" if he re-enters it, to be "on duty" again, and so on.

III.

To begin the game, the owner of Castle No. 1 places and plays his soldier, and then plays his sentinel; then the owner of Castle No. 2, and so on. Each player has to bring his soldier out of his castle (by playing it through the gate), and with it "invade" the other castles in order (e.g., No. 3 has to invade castles 4, 1, 2), re-enter his own castle, and lastly, touch his peg, his sentinel being "on duty" at the time; and whoever does all this first wins. To "invade" a castle, the soldier must enter at the gate, go through the door (either way), touch the peg, and go out at the gate again.

IV.

If an invading soldier touch, or be touched by, the sentinel "on duty" of the castle he is invading, he becomes "prisoner," and is placed behind the peg. He may be released by the sentinel going "off duty," or by his own sentinel "on duty" coming and touching the peg: in the latter case, his sentinel is at once replaced as at the beginning of the game. The released soldier is "in hand" till his next turn, when he is placed as at the beginning of the game.

V.

When a soldier goes through an arch, or touches a peg, "in order," or when a sentinel takes a prisoner, he may be played again. Also when a sentinel leaves, or re-enters, his castle, he may be played again, but may not exercise either of these privileges twice in one turn.

VI.

If the ball played touch another (neither of them being a sentinel "on duty"), the player may "take two" off the ball so touched, but must not move it in doing so. If, however, the ball so touched be his own sentinel "off duty," he may take a croquet of any kind, as in the ordinary game. He may not "take two," or take a croquet twice in one turn off the same ball, unless he has meanwhile gone through an arch, or touched a peg "in order."

N.B. The following arrangement of the 8 balls as soldiers and sentinels will be found convenient:

Castle	*Soldier*	*Sentinel*
I.	Blue	Pink
II.	Black	Yellow
III.	Brown	Orange
IV.	Green	Red

ADVICE TO THE PLAYER

As it is not easy, in a new game, to see at once what is the best method of play in the various situations that may occur, the following suggestions may be of use to the player.

There are two distinct methods of play, which you may adopt in this game, and each has its own special advantages: the one consists in keeping your sentinel "on duty;" the other, in bringing it "off duty."

In the first method, your sentinel remains constantly at home, except when your soldier is in danger of being taken prisoner, when it is played up to the peg of the castle you are invading, so as to be ready to release your soldier. In this method, the best position for your sentinel is opposite to the centre of your gate, and a ball's width from it, so that if a soldier, trying to invade your castle, should touch it, it must have previously passed through the gate. From this position it is easy to take a prisoner in any part of your castle by the following rule:—Play your sentinel just through the gate; this gives you another turn, in which you play it in again, getting as near as possible to the invading soldier; this gives you another turn, in which you may take it prisoner. The same process may be employed for playing your sentinel up to the peg of the castle you are invading, if it should happen that you cannot play it straight for the peg. This process, however, must not be employed when you have a prisoner in your castle, as it would be released by your sentinel going out.

In the second method, your sentinel keeps with your soldier: when playing your soldier, you carry the sentinel along with it, through one or more arches, by raking "loose croquets" or "split strokes;" and when your soldier can do no more, you either play your sentinel close up to it, ready for the next turn, or, if your soldier is in danger of being taken prisoner, you "take two" off it, getting as close as possible to the enemy's sentinel in the first stroke, and driving it to a safe distance in the second.

The first method is the safest, when any one of the other players is better than yourself, as it enables you to prevent his entering your castle and so to delay him; but as soon as all the players, whom you have reason to fear, have passed through your castle, you had better bring your sentinel "off duty," and help your soldier.

The second method enables you to make rapid progress in invading the other castles: you can also take prisoners almost as easily as in the first method, by "taking two" off your soldier, getting near your gate in the first stroke, and entering your castle in the second: this gives you another turn, in which you may take a prisoner. It has, however, the disadvantage of loss of time if your soldier should be made a prisoner, as in this case your sentinel has to go home, get "on duty," and return, before it can release your soldier.

If your soldier is taken prisoner, and you release it by touching the enemy's peg with your sentinel, you are in a position in which you may often retard the other players: first, by placing your sentinel (which is done directly after the release) in a line between your peg and an invading soldier which is aiming at it; secondly, by placing your soldier (which is done when your next turn comes) close to your sentinel, playing it so as to drive your sentinel in the direction of an invading soldier, and then taking it prisoner.

It evidently follows from this that, when you have yourself taken a prisoner, and happen to be invading the castle from which it came, you should not wait till the enemy's sentinel has touched your peg and so released the prisoner, but you should yourself release it (as soon as the enemy's sentinel has nearly reached your peg) by playing your own sentinel out through your gate and in again: in this case the sentinel, which was on its way to your peg, cannot be carried back at once, but must be played all the way home.

In "taking two" off a ball you may, if you choose, play your own ball so as only just to move it, and then strike it in the direction of the other, and thus drive it to a distance. This has nearly the same effect as the "loose croquet" of the ordinary game, but with this difference, that it does not give you the right of playing again.

If a soldier, about to invade your castle, is lying near your gate, you may take it prisoner thus: Play your sentinel out, near the soldier; then hit it with your sentinel, and "take two" off it, so as only just to move your ball, taking care to have the soldier in a line between your sentinel and your gate; then drive both in together; this gives you another turn, in which you may take it prisoner.

Sitting in a Circle

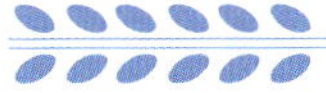

The following mathematical puzzle appeared in Lewis Carroll's 1895 book *Pillow-Problems*. There are 72 problems in the book, which Carroll solved in his head while lying awake at night, hence the title. This is an interesting, but difficult, puzzle to solve, so you have been warned!

Some men sat in a circle, so that each had 2 neighbours and each had a certain number of shillings. The first had 1 shilling more than the second, who had 1 shilling more than the third, and so on.

The first gave 1 shilling to the second, who gave 2 shillings to the third, and so on, each giving 1 shilling more than he received, as long as possible. There were then 2 neighbours, one of whom had 4 times as much as the other.

1. How many men were there?

2. And how much had the poorest man at first?

What's in the Bag?

Here is another problem from Lewis Carroll's book of mathematical puzzles *Pillow-Problems*. It is also fiendishly tricky and you will need a good amount of mathematical knowledge to solve it.

There are two bags, one containing a counter, known to be either white or black; the other containing 1 white and 2 black. A white is put into the first, the bag shaken, and a counter drawn out, which proves to be white. Which course will now give the best chance of drawing a white – to draw from one of the two bags without knowing which it is, or to empty one bag into the other and then draw?

Queen Alice

EXCERPT FROM *Through the Looking-Glass*, Chapter 9

The White Queen and Red Queen invite Alice to her own dinner party and interrogate her with nonsensical questions.

'Manners are not taught in lessons,' said Alice. 'Lessons teach you to do sums, and things of that sort.'

'Can you do Addition?' the White Queen asked. 'What's one and one and one and one and one and one and one and one and one and one?'

'I don't know,' said Alice. 'I lost count.'

'She can't do Addition,' the Red Queen interrupted. 'Can you do Subtraction? Take nine from eight.'

'Nine from eight I can't, you know,' Alice replied very readily; 'but—'

'She can't do Subtraction,' said the White Queen. 'Can you do Division? Divide a loaf by a knife – what's the answer to *that*?'

'I suppose—' Alice was beginning, but the Red Queen answered for her. 'Bread-and-butter, of course. Try another Subtraction sum. Take a bone from a dog. What remains?'

Alice considered. 'The bone wouldn't remain, of course, if I took it – and the dog wouldn't remain; it would come to bite me

– and I'm sure *I* shouldn't remain!'

'Then you think nothing would remain?' said the Red Queen.

'I think that's the answer.'

'Wrong, as usual,' said the Red Queen; 'the dog's temper would remain.'

'But I don't see how—'

'Why, look here!' the Red Queen cried. 'The dog would lose its temper, wouldn't it?'

'Perhaps it would,' Alice replied cautiously.

'Then if the dog went away, its temper would remain!' the Queen exclaimed.

Alice said, as gravely as she could, 'They might go different ways.' But she couldn't help thinking to herself, 'What dreadful nonsense we *are* talking!'

'She can't do sums a *bit*!' the Queens said together, with great emphasis.

'Can *you* do sums?' Alice said, turning suddenly on the White Queen, for she didn't like being found fault with so much.

The Queen gasped and shut her eyes. 'I can do Addition,' she said, 'if you give me time – but I can't do Subtraction under *any* circumstances!'

Cat Feeding

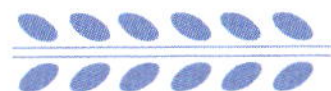

This is the fifth verse riddle in Lewis Carroll's 'Puzzles from Wonderland'. Why did the cat refuse to eat the offering from the third sister? The answer is hidden in the verse.

Three sisters at breakfast were feeding the cat.
The first gave it sole – Puss was grateful for that:
The next gave it salmon – which Puss thought a treat:
The third gave it herring – which Puss wouldn't eat.

The King and his Wise Men

Here is another verse riddle devised by Lewis Carroll for 'Puzzles from Wonderland'. Can you work out how many Wise Men the King kept?

When the King found that his money was nearly all gone, and that he really *must* live more economically, he decided on sending away most of his Wise Men. There were some hundreds of them – very fine old men, and magnificently dressed in green velvet gowns with gold buttons: if they *had* a fault, it was that they always contradicted one another when he asked for their advice – and they certainly ate and drank *enormously*. So, on the whole, he was rather glad to get rid of them. But there was an old law, which he did not dare to disobey, which said that there must always be

'Seven blind of both eyes:
Ten blind of one eye:
Five that see with both eyes:
Nine that see with one eye.'

DOUBLETS

The main rules for solving Doublets are on page 54.

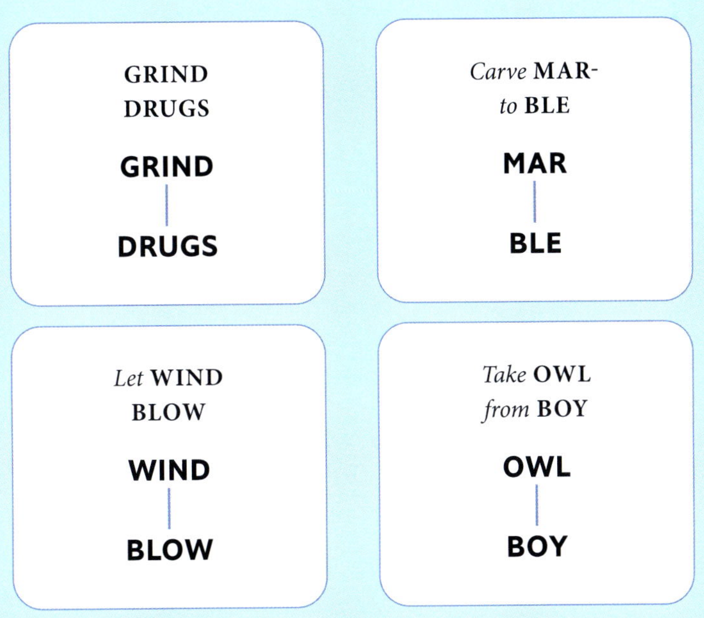

Go from NORTH *to* SOUTH

NORTH

|

SOUTH

Plant ALOE *on* BANK

ALOE

|

BANK

Prove that a BIPED WALKS

BIPED

|

WALKS

DREAM *of* STARS

DREAM

|

STARS

Connect FOUR TEEN

FOUR

|

TEEN

Build CAS-TLE

CAS

|

TLE

Tame EAG-LES

EAG

|

LES

SEEK *and* FIND

SEEK

|

FIND

Turn CALF
into VEAL
CALF
VEAL
PULL
PLUG
PULL
PLUG
A SOLU-
TION
SOLU
TION
WRITE
POEMS
WRITE
POEMS
ENTER
HAVEN
ENTER
HAVEN
Make LOVER
HAPPY
LOVER
HAPPY
MIX
TEA
MIX
TEA
SPIN
COIN
SPIN
COIN

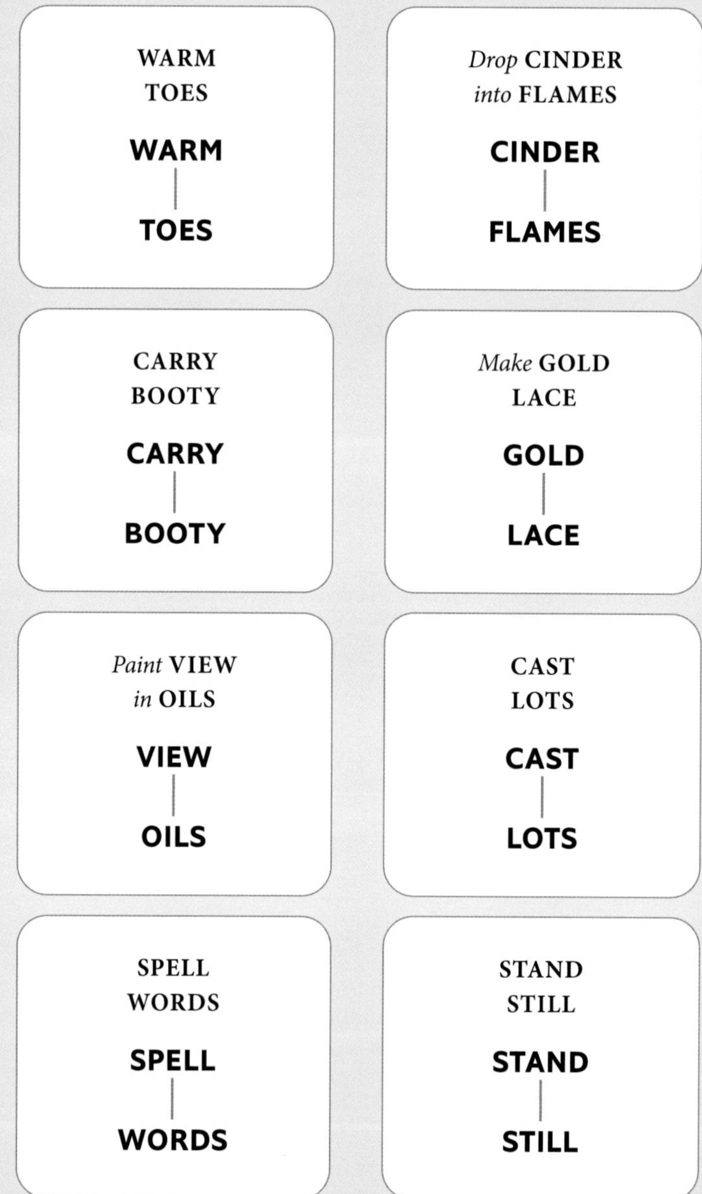
WARM
TOES
WARM
TOES
Drop CINDER
into FLAMES
CINDER
FLAMES
CARRY
BOOTY
CARRY
BOOTY
Make GOLD
LACE
GOLD
LACE
Paint VIEW
in OILS
VIEW
OILS
CAST
LOTS
CAST
LOTS
SPELL
WORDS
SPELL
WORDS
STAND
STILL
STAND
STILL

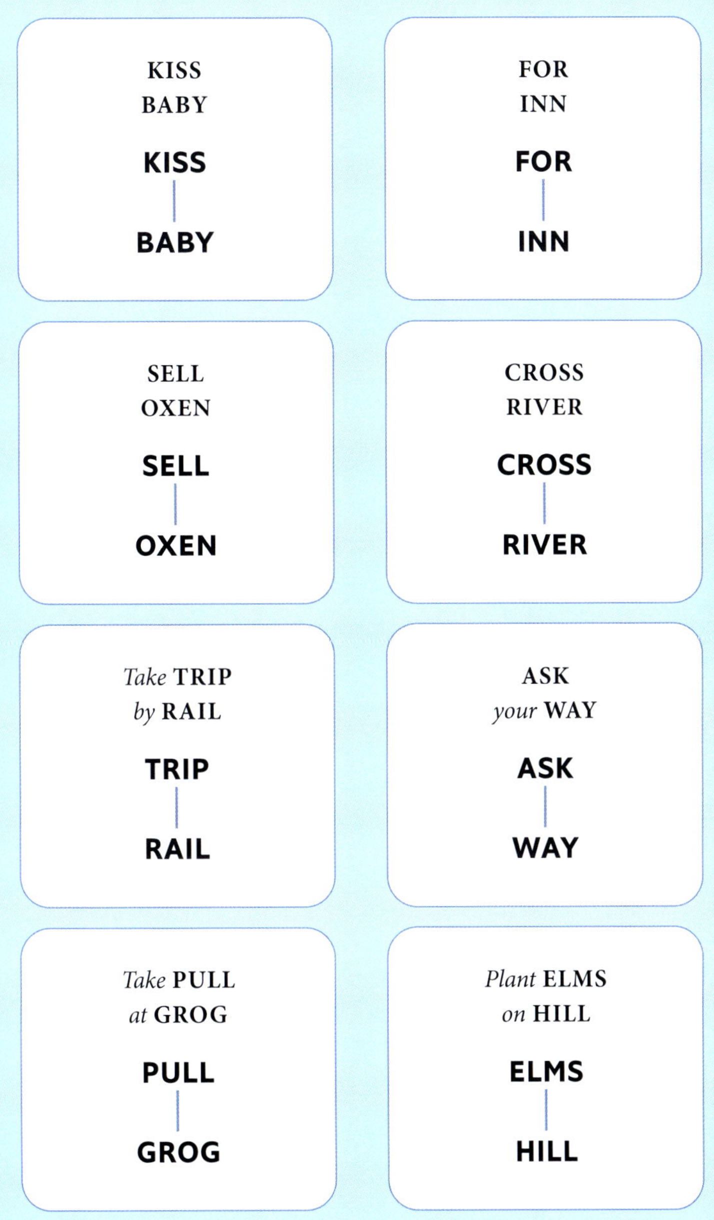

KISS
BABY
KISS
BABY
FOR
INN
FOR
INN
SELL
OXEN
SELL
OXEN
CROSS
RIVER
CROSS
RIVER
Take TRIP
by RAIL
TRIP
RAIL
ASK
your WAY
ASK
WAY
Take PULL
at GROG
PULL
GROG
Plant ELMS
on HILL
ELMS
HILL

Cure CRABS
of SLOTH

CRABS
|
SLOTH

Set WREN
on NEST

WREN
|
NEST

CHECK
NOISE

CHECK
|
NOISE

COURT
WORLD

COURT
|
WORLD

Send GREEKS
to CRIMEA

GREEKS
|
CRIMEA

BREAK
CHINA

BREAK
|
CHINA

WHY *make much*
ADO?

WHY
|
ADO

FRY
APE

FRY
|
APE

SHUT
EYES
SHUT
EYES
DUST
ROOM
DUST
ROOM
Light GAS
at EVE
GAS
EVE
CLASP
CLOAK
CLASP
CLOAK
WEAR
GEMS
WEAR
GEMS
Spend DAY
on ICE
DAY
ICE
BRING
PEACE
BRING
PEACE
Change BEER
for WINE
BEER
WINE

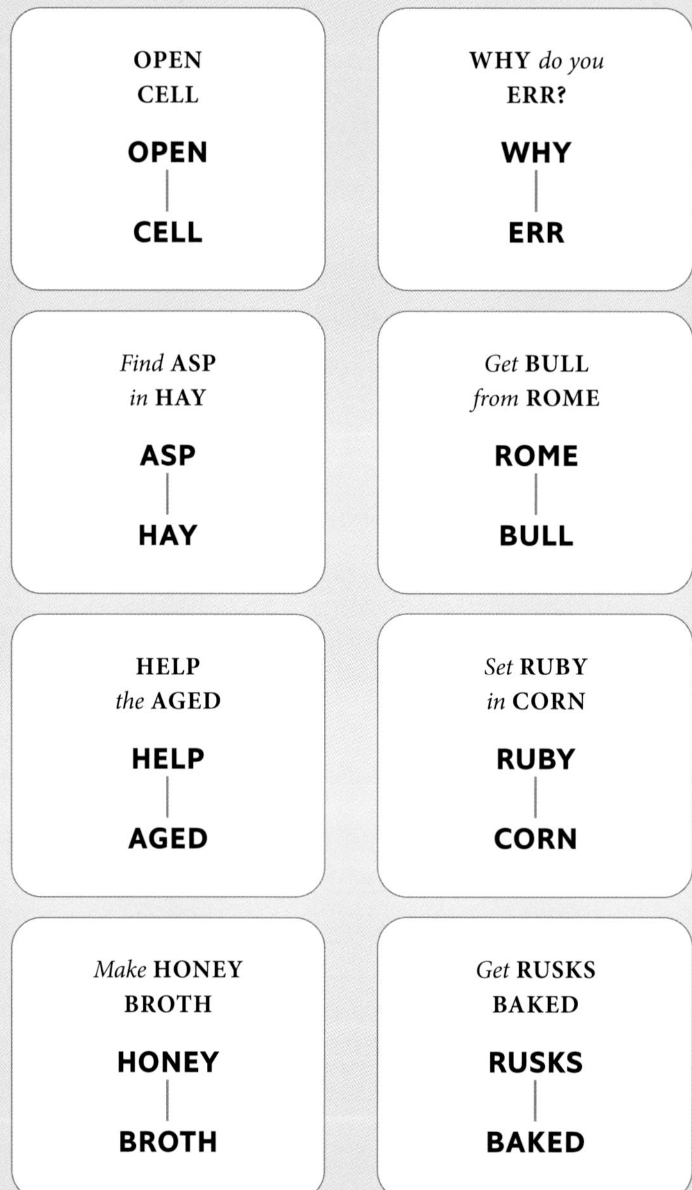

OPEN
CELL
OPEN
CELL
WHY *do you*
ERR?
WHY
ERR
Find ASP
in HAY
ASP
HAY
Get BULL
from ROME
ROME
BULL
HELP
the AGED
HELP
AGED
Set RUBY
in CORN
RUBY
CORN
Make HONEY
BROTH
HONEY
BROTH
Get RUSKS
BAKED
RUSKS
BAKED

Feed BULL *on* FIGS
BULL
FIGS
Heal DISC-ORDS
DISC
ORDS
YELL *at* IBIS
YELL
IBIS
Run AWL *into* WAX
AWL
WAX
CRY 'AYE!'
CRY
AYE
ROAST DUCKS
ROAST
DUCKS
KEEP OATH
KEEP
OATH
Keep ANT *in* BOX
ANT
BOX

Find APEX
of CONE

CONE
|
APEX

Crown TIGER
with ROSES

TIGER
|
ROSES

Mix CURDS
and CREAM

CURDS
|
CREAM

Pay COSTS
in PENCE

COSTS
|
PENCE

REST *on*
SOFA

REST
|
SOFA

Raise ONE
to TWO

ONE
|
TWO

Sell SHOES
for CRUST

SHOES
|
CRUST

Change BLUE
to PINK

BLUE
|
PINK

Missing Unit

The Lewis Carroll Picture Book (1899) features a puzzle similar to this. In the diagram below, the four pieces that make up the square on the left have been rearranged to make the rectangle on the right. But look closely, the square has an area of 64 units, yet the rectangle has an area of 65 units.

Where does the extra unit come from?

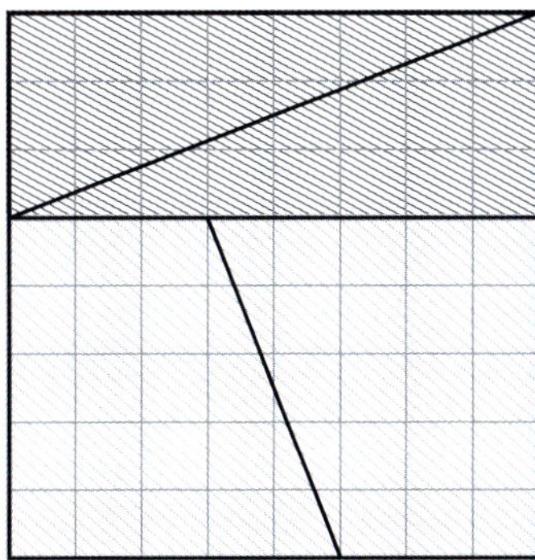

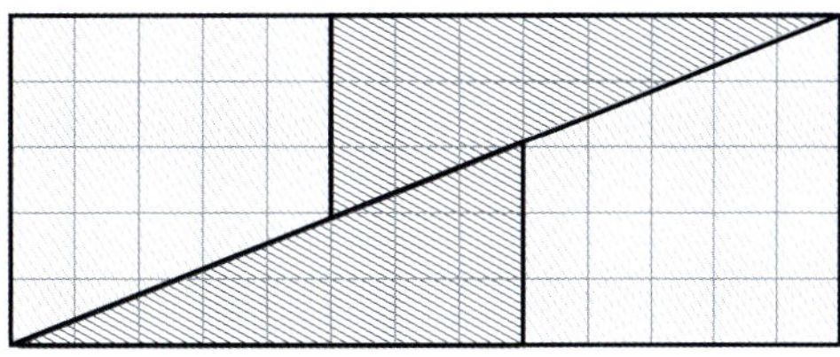

Hidden Name

This acrostic poem, which appears at the beginning of Lewis Carroll's *A Tangled Tale* is dedicated to one of his child-friends. The name is hidden within the poem – can you find it?

TO MY PUPIL

Beloved Pupil! Tamed by thee,
Addish-, Subtrac-, Multiplica-tion,
Division, Fractions, Rule of Three,
Attest thy deft manipulation!

Then onward! Let the voice of fame
from Age to Age repeat thy story,
Till thou hast won thyself a name
Exceeding even Euclid's glory!

Double Acrostic

This dedicatory poem appears at the beginning of Lewis Carroll's epic nonsense book *The Hunting of the Snark*. It is a double acrostic because a name appears twice in the poem – can you see where?

Girt with a boyish garb for boyish task,
   Eager she wields her spade: yet loves as well
Rest on a friendly knee, intent to ask
   The tale he loves to tell.

Rude spirits of the seething outer strife,
   Unmeet to read her pure and simple spright,
Deem, if you list, such hours a waste of life,
   Empty of all delight!

Chat on, sweet Maid, and rescue from annoy
   Hearts that by wiser talk are unbeguiled.
Ah, happy he who owns that tenderest joy,
   The heart-love of a child!

Away, fond thoughts, and vex my soul no more!
  Work claims my wakeful nights, my busy days –
Albeit bright memories of that sunlit shore
  Yet haunt my dreaming gaze!

The Fish Riddle

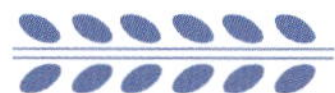

EXCERPT FROM *Through the Looking-Glass*, Chapter 9

The White Queen recites a poem to Alice. Can you guess what the fish-dish is?

'As to fishes,' she said, very slowly and solemnly, putting her mouth close to Alice's ear, 'her White Majesty knows a lovely riddle – all in poetry – all about fishes. Shall she repeat it?'

'Her Red Majesty's very kind to mention it,' the White Queen murmured into Alice's other ear, in a voice like the cooing of a pigeon. 'It would be such *a treat! May I?'*

'Please do,' Alice said very politely.

The White Queen laughed with delight, and stroked Alice's cheek. Then she began:

'"First the fish must be caught."
That is easy: a baby, I think, could have caught it.
"Next, the fish must be bought."
That is easy: a penny, I think, would have bought it.

"Now cook me the fish!"
That is easy, and will not take more than a minute.
"Let it lie in a dish!"
That is easy, because it already is in it.

"Bring it here! Let me sup!"
It is easy to set such a dish on the table.
"Take the dish-cover up!"
Ah, *that* is so hard that I fear I'm unable!

For it holds it like glue –
Holds the lid to the dish, while it lies in the middle:
Which is easiest to do,
Un-dish-cover the fish, or dishcover the riddle?'

'Take a minute to think about it, and then guess.'

Rebus Letter

In 1869, Lewis Carroll sent Georgina Watson an illustrated letter to explain why he could not be with her on her birthday. It's a rebus letter, in which pictures replace some of the words. Can you decipher its contents?

The

My Ina,

Though don't give
birthday presents, still
April
. . . write a birthday .
June
came 2 your 2
wish U many happy returns
of the day, the met
me, took me for a ,
hunted me and
till could hardly
However somehow got
into the , there
a met me, took me
for a , and pelted me

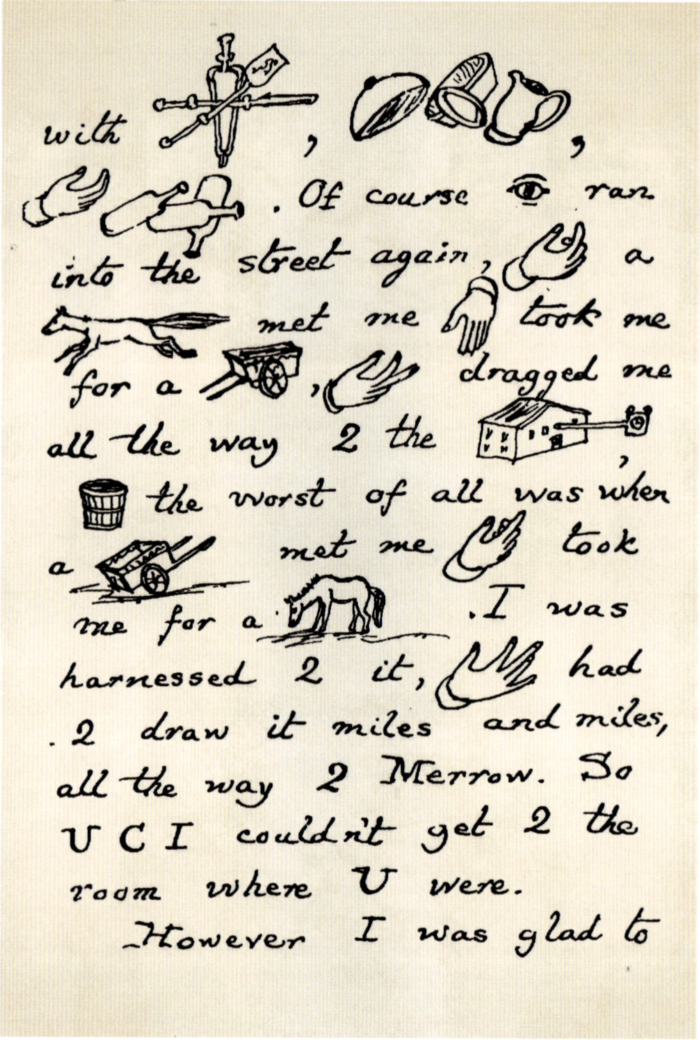

with , ,
. Of course ran
into the street again, a
met me took me
for a , dragged me
all the way 2 the ,
the worst of all was when
a met me took
me for a . I was
harnessed 2 it, had
. 2 draw it miles and miles,
all the way 2 Merrow. So
U C I couldn't get 2 the
room where U were.

However I was glad to

hear U were hard at work
learning the

	2	3	4	5
2	4	6	8	10
3	6	9	12	15
4	8	12	16	20
5	10	15	20	25

for a
birthday treat.

I had just time 2 look
into the kitchen, and
your birthday feast
getting ready, a nice
of crusts, bones, pills,
cotton-bobbins, and rhubarb
and magnesia- "Now," I
thought, "she will be happy!"
and with a I went
on my way.

Your aff^te friend

CLD

The Hunting of the Snark

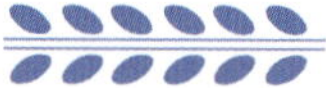

Mathematical ideas are featured in the epic nonsense poem *The Hunting of the Snark*, including the arithmetical reasoning below proposed by a member of the ship's crew, the Butcher.

So engrossed was the Butcher, he heeded them not,
As he wrote with a pen in each hand,
And explained all the while in a popular style
Which the Beaver could well understand.
'Taking Three as the subject to reason about –
A convenient number to state –
We add Seven, and Ten, and then multiply out
By One Thousand diminished by Eight.
'The result we proceed to divide, as you see,
By Nine Hundred and Ninety Two:
Then subtract Seventeen, and the answer must be
Exactly and perfectly true.
'The method employed I would gladly explain,

While I have it so clear in my head,
If I had but the time and you had but the brain –
While I have it so clear in my head,
But much yet remains to be said.

What is the answer? What happens if you try with other answers?

Alphabet Cipher

Lewis Carroll invented this cipher in 1868 – it facilitates the sending of coded messages. The sender uses a keyword to decode a message and the receiver who also knows the keyword reverses the process to recover the original message.

See if you can decode this extract using the cipher – there are instructions on how to do that overleaf.

The keyword is: CATERPILLAR.

UHX WKGMENHVF HXVJTTQ FP FP TBTKDM, LYD GGEIIU DDPC TYG EWKV DN ESE DWSAVFDU, LYD YGR XCVH QXXEUKAMICN UPE TYQSX SW P TLCGV DLNI TPBPCPZNLTV, KWIE HAJ UIMXZCO ZY TYG THT, NXBS TTJ CRFW WDTOPD, HWIXXCN AXZKZPG T PFCO SZOBCH, TRU IIVTNX POM XYT AXLLCGSM RFIQNP OW JEK SI DN LYYKJIGK VAAP.

	A	B	C	D	E	F	G	H	I	J	K	L	M	N	O	P	Q	R	S	T	U	V	W	X	Y	Z
A	a	b	c	d	e	f	g	h	i	j	k	l	m	n	o	p	q	r	s	t	u	v	w	x	y	z
B	b	c	d	e	f	g	h	i	j	k	l	m	n	o	p	q	r	s	t	u	v	w	x	y	z	a
C	c	d	e	f	g	h	i	j	k	l	m	n	o	p	q	r	s	t	u	v	w	x	y	z	a	b
D	d	e	f	g	h	i	j	k	l	m	n	o	p	q	r	s	t	u	v	w	x	y	z	a	b	c
E	e	f	g	h	i	j	k	l	m	n	o	p	q	r	s	t	u	v	w	x	y	z	a	b	c	d
F	f	g	h	i	j	k	l	m	n	o	p	q	r	s	t	u	v	w	x	y	z	a	b	c	d	e
G	g	h	i	j	k	l	m	n	o	p	q	r	s	t	u	v	w	x	y	z	a	b	c	d	e	f
H	h	i	j	k	l	m	n	o	p	q	r	s	t	u	v	w	x	y	z	a	b	c	d	e	f	g
I	i	j	k	l	m	n	o	p	q	r	s	t	u	v	w	x	y	z	a	b	c	d	e	f	g	h
J	j	k	l	m	n	o	p	q	r	s	t	u	v	w	x	y	z	a	b	c	d	e	f	g	h	i
K	k	l	m	n	o	p	q	r	s	t	u	v	w	x	y	z	a	b	c	d	e	f	g	h	i	j
L	l	m	n	o	p	q	r	s	t	u	v	w	x	y	z	a	b	c	d	e	f	g	h	i	j	k
M	m	n	o	p	q	r	s	t	u	v	w	x	y	z	a	b	c	d	e	f	g	h	i	j	k	l
N	n	o	p	q	r	s	t	u	v	w	x	y	z	a	b	c	d	e	f	g	h	i	j	k	l	m
O	o	p	q	r	s	t	u	v	w	x	y	z	a	b	c	d	e	f	g	h	i	j	k	l	m	n
P	p	q	r	s	t	u	v	w	x	y	z	a	b	c	d	e	f	g	h	i	j	k	l	m	n	o
Q	q	r	s	t	u	v	w	x	y	z	a	b	c	d	e	f	g	h	i	j	k	l	m	n	o	p
R	r	s	t	u	v	w	x	y	z	a	b	c	d	e	f	g	h	i	j	k	l	m	n	o	p	q
S	s	t	u	v	w	x	y	z	a	b	c	d	e	f	g	h	i	j	k	l	m	n	o	p	q	r
T	t	u	v	w	x	y	z	a	b	c	d	e	f	g	h	i	j	k	l	m	n	o	p	q	r	s
U	u	v	w	x	y	z	a	b	c	d	e	f	g	h	i	j	k	l	m	n	o	p	q	r	s	t
V	v	w	x	y	z	a	b	c	d	e	f	g	h	i	j	k	l	m	n	o	p	q	r	s	t	u
W	w	x	y	z	a	b	c	d	e	f	g	h	i	j	k	l	m	n	o	p	q	r	s	t	u	v
X	x	y	z	a	b	c	d	e	f	g	h	i	j	k	l	m	n	o	p	q	r	s	t	u	v	w
Y	y	z	a	b	c	d	e	f	g	h	i	j	k	l	m	n	o	p	q	r	s	t	u	v	w	x
Z	z	a	b	c	d	e	f	g	h	i	j	k	l	m	n	o	p	q	r	s	t	u	v	w	x	y

To decode the extract repeatedly write the keyword above the letters of the coded extract.

c a t e r p i l l a r c a t e
U H X W K G M E N H V F H X V

Then use the alphabet grid to decode the message as follows:

1. Find the letter in the keyword along the top row of the grid (an uppercase letter).
2. Look down that column, until you find the corresponding letter in the encoded message (a lowercase letter in the grid).
3. Move along this row to the far left, to the uppercase letter in the first column. This is the decoded letter.

For example, to decode the first letter of the extract 'U', we find the first letter of the keyword 'C' in the top row of the grid, move down until we find 'u' in this column, then move to the left of the row and read the uppercase letter 'S'. So 'S' is the first letter of the decoded message.

Twiddle Your Eyes

EXCERPT FROM *Sylvie and Bruno Concluded*, Chapter 1

Sylvie was arranging some letters on a board—E—V—I—L. 'Now, Bruno,' she said, 'what does that spell?'

Bruno looked at it, in solemn silence, for a minute. 'I knows what it doesn't *spell!' he said at last.*

'That's no good,' said Sylvie. 'What does *it spell?'*

Bruno took another look at the mysterious letters. 'Why, it's "LIVE," backwards!' he exclaimed. (I thought it was, indeed.)

'How did *you manage to see that?' said Sylvie.*

'I just twiddled my eyes,' said Bruno, 'and then I saw it directly.'

In 1892 Lewis Carroll invented what he thought was a new kind of riddle. Here is the problem – the above extract may help you solve it.

A Russian had three sons.
The first, named Rab, became a lawyer.
The second, Ymra, became a soldier.
The third became a sailor: what was his name?

A TANGLED TALE

"A knot!" said Alice, always ready to make herself useful, and looking about her. "Oh, do let me help to undo it!"

Beginning in 1884 Lewis Carroll wrote ten stories which concealed an intriguing mathematical problem. Each story was called a 'knot' and were published in a book entitled *A Tangled Tale* with illustrations by A. B. Frost. Here are the first three stories.

Carroll provided summaries of the problems, as well as solutions and answers, and these are provided on page 187.

A.B.F.

KNOT I

EXCELSIOR

"Goblin, lead them up and down."

THE ruddy glow of sunset was already fading into the sombre shadows of night, when two travellers might have been observed swiftly – at a pace of six miles in the hour – descending the rugged side of a mountain; the younger bounding from crag to crag with the agility of a fawn, while his companion, whose aged limbs seemed ill at ease in the heavy chain armour habitually worn by tourists in that district, toiled on painfully at his side.

As is always the case under such circumstances, the younger knight was the first to break the silence.

"A goodly pace, I trow!" he exclaimed. "We sped not thus in the ascent!"

"Goodly, indeed!" the other echoed with a groan, "We climb it but at three miles in the hour."

"And on the dead level our pace is—?" the younger suggested; for he was weak in statistics, and left all such details to his aged companion.

"Four miles in the hour," the other wearily replied. "Not an ounce more," he added, with that love of metaphor so common in old age, "and not a farthing less!"

" 'Twas three hours past high noon when we left our hostelry," the young man said, musingly. "We shall scarce be back by supper-time. Perchance mine host will roundly deny us all food!"

"He will chide our tardy return," was the grave reply, "and such a rebuke will be meet."

"A brave conceit!" cried the other, with a merry laugh. "And should we bid him bring us yet another course, I trow his answer will be tart!"

"We shall but get our deserts," sighed the elder knight, who had never seen a joke in his life, and was somewhat displeased at his companion's untimely levity. " 'Twill be nine of the clock," he added in an undertone, "by the time we regain our hostelry. Full many a mile shall we have plodded this day!"

"How many? How many?" cried the eager youth, ever a thirst for knowledge.

The old man was silent.

"Tell me," he answered, after a moment's thought, "what time it was when we stood together on yonder peak. Not exact to the minute!" he added hastily, reading a protest in the young man's face. "An' thy guess be within one poor half-hour of the mark, 'tis all I ask of thy mother's son! Then will I tell thee, true to the last inch, how far we shall have trudged betwixt three and nine of the clock."

A groan was the young man's only reply; while his convulsed features and the deep wrinkles that chased each other across his manly brow, revealed the abyss of arithmetical agony into which one chance question had plunged him.

KNOT II

ELIGIBLE APARTMENTS

"Straight down the crooked lane,
And all round the square."

"LET'S ask Balbus about it," said Hugh.

"All right," said Lambert.

"He can guess it," said Hugh.

"Rather," said Lambert.

No more words were needed: the two brothers understood each other perfectly.

Balbus was waiting for them at the hotel: the journey down had tired him, he said: so his two pupils had been the round of the place, in search of lodgings, without the old tutor who had been their inseparable companion from their childhood. They had named him after the hero of their Latin exercise-book, which overflowed with anecdotes of that versatile genius – anecdotes whose vagueness in detail was more than compensated by their sensational brilliance. "Balbus has overcome all his enemies" had been marked by their tutor, in the margin of the book, "Successful Bravery." In this way he had tried to extract a moral from every anecdote about Balbus – sometimes one of warning, as in "Balbus had borrowed a healthy dragon," against which he

A.B.F.
SWAIN Sc

had written "Rashness in Speculation" – sometimes of encouragement, as in the words "Influence of Sympathy in United Action," which stood opposite to the anecdote "Balbus was assisting his mother-in-law to convince the dragon" – and sometimes it dwindled down to a single word such as "Prudence," which was all he could extract from the touching record that "Balbus, having scorched the tail of the dragon, went away." His pupils liked the short morals best, as it left them more room for marginal illustrations, and in this instance they required all the space they could get to exhibit the rapidity of the hero's departure.

Their report of the state of things was discouraging. That most fashionable of watering-places, Little Mendip, was "chockfull" (as the boys expressed it) from end to end. But in one Square they had seen no less than four cards, in different houses, all announcing in flaming capitals "ELIGIBLE APARTMENTS." "So there's plenty of choice, after all, you see," said spokesman Hugh in conclusion.

"That doesn't follow from the data," said Balbus, as he rose from the easy chair, where he had been dozing over *The Little Mendip Gazette*. "They may be all single rooms. However, we may as well see them. I shall be glad to stretch my legs a bit."

An unprejudiced bystander might have objected that the operation was needless, and that this long, lank creature would have been all the better with even shorter legs: but no such thought occurred to his loving pupils. One on each side, they did their best to keep up with his gigantic strides, while Hugh repeated the sentence in their father's letter, just received from abroad, over which he and Lambert had been puzzling. "He says a friend of his, the Governor of – *what* was that name again, Lambert?" ("Kgovjni," said Lambert.) "Well, yes. The Governor of – what-you-may-call-it – wants to give a *very* small dinner-party, and he means to ask his father's brother-in-law, his brother's father-in-law, his father-in-law's brother, and his brother-in-law's father: and we're to guess how many guests there will be."

There was an anxious pause. "*How* large did he say the pudding was to be?" Balbus said at last. "Take its cubical contents, divide by the cubical contents of what each man can eat, and the quotient—"

"He didn't say anything about pudding," said Hugh," – and here's the Square," as they turned a corner and came into sight of the "eligible apartments."

"It *is* a Square!" was Balbus' first cry of delight, as he gazed around him. "Beautiful! Beau-ti-ful! Equilateral! And rectangular!"

The boys looked round with less enthusiasm. "Number nine is the first with a card," said prosaic Lambert; but Balbus would not so soon awake from his dream of beauty.

"See, boys!" he cried. "Twenty doors on a side! What symmetry! Each side divided into twenty-one equal parts! It's delicious!"

"Shall I knock, or ring ?" said Hugh, looking in some perplexity at a square brass plate which bore the simple inscription "RING ALSO."

"Both," said Balbus. "That's an Ellipsis, my boy. Did you never see an Ellipsis before?"

"I couldn't hardly read it," said Hugh, evasively. "It's no good having an Ellipsis, if they don't keep it clean."

"Which there is *one* room, gentlemen," said the smiling landlady. "And a sweet room too! As snug a little back-room—"

"We will see it," said Balbus gloomily, as they followed her in. "I knew how it would be! One room in each house! No view, I suppose ?"

"Which indeed there *is*, gentlemen!" the landlady indignantly protested, as she drew up the blind, and indicated the back garden.

"Cabbages, I perceive," said Balbus. "Well, they're green, at any rate."

"Which the greens at the shops, " their hostess explained, "are by no means dependable upon. Here you has them on the premises, *and* of the best."

"Does the window open?" was always Balbus' first question in testing a lodging: and "Does the chimney smoke?" his second. Satisfied on all points, he secured the refusal of the room, and they moved on to Number Twenty-five.

This landlady was grave and stern. "I've nobbut one room left," she told them: "and it gives on the back-gyardin."

"But there are cabbages?" Balbus suggested.

The landlady visibly relented. "There is, sir," she said: "and good ones, though I say it as shouldn't. We can't rely on the shops for greens. So we grows them ourselves."

"A singular advantage," said Balbus: and, after the usual questions, they went on to Fifty-two.

"And I'd gladly accommodate you all, if I could," was the greeting that met them. "We are but mortal." ("Irrelevant!" muttered Balbus) "and I've let all my rooms but one."

"Which one is a back-room, I perceive," said Balbus: "and looking out on – on cabbages, I presume?"

"Yes, indeed, sir !" said their hostess. "Whatever *other* folks may do, *we* grows our own. For the shops—"

"An excellent arrangement!" Balbus interrupted. "Then one can really depend on their being good. Does the window open?"

The usual questions were answered satisfactorily: but this time Hugh added one of his own invention – "Does the cat scratch?"

The landlady looked round suspiciously, as if to make sure the cat was not listening, "I will not deceive you, gentlemen," she said. "It *do* scratch, but not without you pulls its whiskers! It'll never do it," she repeated slowly, with a visible effort to recall the exact words of some written agreement between herself and the cat, "without you pulls its whiskers!"

"Much may be excused in a cat so treated," said Balbus, as they left the house and crossed to Number Seventy-three, leaving the landlady curtseying on the doorstep, and still murmuring to herself her parting words, as if they were a form of blessing, "– not without you pulls its whiskers!"

At Number Seventy-three they found only a small shy girl to show the house, who said "yes'm" in answer to all questions.

"The usual room," said Balbus, as they marched in: "the usual back-garden, the usual cabbages. I suppose you can't get them good at the shops?"

"Yes'm," said the girl.

"Well, you may tell your mistress we will take the room, and that her plan of growing her own cabbages is simply *admirable*!"

"Yes'm," said the girl, as she showed them out.

"One day-room and three bed-rooms," said Balbus, as they returned to the hotel. "We will take as our day-room the one that gives us the least walking to do to get to it."

"Must we walk from door to door, and count the steps?" said Lambert.

"No, no! Figure it out, my boys, figure it out!" Balbus gaily exclaimed, as he put pens, ink, and paper before his hapless pupils, and left the room.

"I say! It'll be a job!" said Hugh.

"Rather!" said Lambert.

KNOT III

MAD MATHESIS

"I waited for the train."

"WELL, they call me so because I *am* a little mad, I suppose," she said, good-humouredly, in answer to Clara's cautiously-worded question as to how she came by so strange a nick-name. "You see, I never do what sane people are expected to do now-a-days. I never wear long trains, (talking of trains, that's the Charing Cross Metropolitan Station – I've something to tell you about *that*), and I never play lawn-tennis. I can't cook an omelette. I can't even set a broken limb! *There's* an ignoramus for you!"

Clara was her niece, and full twenty years her junior; in fact, she was still attending a High School – an institution of which Mad Mathesis spoke with undisguised aversion. "Let a woman be meek and lowly!" she would say. "None of your High Schools for me!" But it was vacation time just now, and Clara was her guest, and Mad Mathesis was showing her the sights of that Eighth Wonder of the world – London.

"The Charing Cross Metropolitan Station!" she resumed, waving her hand towards the entrance as if she were introducing her niece to a friend. "The Bayswater and Birmingham Extension is just completed, and the trains now run round and round continuously – skirting the border of Wales, just touching at York, and so round by the east coast back to London. The way the trains run is *most* peculiar. The westerly ones go round in two hours; the easterly ones take three; but they always manage to start two trains from here, opposite ways, punctually every quarter-of-an-hour."

"They part to meet again," said Clara, her eyes filling with tears at the romantic thought.

"No need to cry about it!" her aunt grimly remarked. "They don't meet on the same line of rails, you know. Talking of meeting, an idea strikes me!" she added, changing the subject with her usual abruptness. "Let's go opposite ways round, and see which can meet most trains. No need for a chaperon – ladies' saloon, you know. You shall go whichever way you like, and we'll have a bet about it!"

"I never make bets," Clara said very gravely. "Our excellent preceptress has often warned us—"

"You'd be none the worse if you did!" Mad Mathesis interrupted. "In fact, you'd be the better, I'm certain!"

"Neither does our excellent preceptress approve of puns," said Clara. "But we'll have a match, if you like. Let me choose my train, she added after a brief mental calculation, "and I'll engage to meet exactly half as many again as you do."

"Not if you count fair," Mad Mathesis bluntly interrupted. "Remember, we only count the trains we meet *on the way*. You mustn't count the one that starts as you start, nor the one that arrives as you arrive."

"That will only make the difference of *one* train," said Clara, as they turned and entered the station. "But I never travelled alone before. There'll be no one to help me to alight. However, I don't mind. Let's have a match."

A ragged little boy overheard her remark, and came running after her.

"Buy a box of cigar lights, Miss!" he pleaded, pulling her shawl to attract her attention. Clara stopped to explain.

"I never smoke cigars," she said in a meekly apologetic tone. "Our excellent preceptress—," but Mad Mathesis impatiently hurried her on, and the little boy was left gazing after her with round eyes of amazement.

The two ladies bought their tickets and moved slowly down the central platform, Mad Mathesis prattling on as usual – Clara silent, anxiously reconsidering the calculation on which she rested her hopes of winning the match.

"Mind where you go, dear!" cried her aunt, checking her just in time. "One step more, and you'd have been in that pail of cold water!"

"I know, I know, " Clara said, dreamily. "The pale, the cold, and the moony—"

"Take your places on the spring-boards!" shouted a porter.

"What are *they* for!" Clara asked in a terrified whisper.

"Merely to help us into the trains." The elder lady spoke with the nonchalance of one quite used to the process. "Very few people can get into a carriage without help in less than three seconds, and the trains only stop for one second." At this moment the whistle was heard, and two trains rushed into the station. A moment's pause, and they were gone again; but in that brief interval several hundred passengers had been shot into them, each flying straight to his place with the accuracy of a Minie bullet – while an equal number were showered out upon the side-platforms.

Three hours had passed away, and the two friends met again on the Charing Cross platform, and eagerly compared notes. Then Clara turned away with a sigh. To young impulsive hearts, like hers, disappointment is always a bitter pill. Mad Mathesis followed her, full of kindly sympathy.

"Try again, my love!" she said, cheerily. "Let us vary the experiment. We will start as we did before, but not to begin counting till our trains meet. When we see each other, we will say 'One!' and so count on till we come here again."

Clara brightened up. "I shall win *that,*" she exclaimed eagerly, "if I may choose my train!"

Another shriek of engine whistles, another up-heaving of spring-boards, another living avalanche plunging into two trains as they flashed by: and the travellers were off again.

Each gazed eagerly from her carriage window, holding up her handkerchief as a signal to her friend. A rush and a roar. Two trains shot past each other in a tunnel, and two travellers leaned back in their corners with a sigh – or rather with *two* sighs – of relief. "One!" Clara murmured to herself. "Won! It's a word of good omen. *This* time, at any rate, the victory will be mine!"

But *was* it?

OMNIBUSES AND CHELSEA PENSIONERS

Here are two problems hidden in Knots VIII and Knot X of *A Tangled Tale*, summarised by Lewis Carroll. The first problem is about the timing of omnibuses (buses).

1. Omnibuses start from a certain point, both ways, every 15 minutes. A traveller, starting on foot along with one of them, meets one in 12½ minutes: when will he be overtaken by one?

The second problem relates to Chelsea Pensioners, retired soldiers of the British army, and their respective war wounds

2. If 70 per cent have lost an eye, 75 per cent, an ear, 80 per cent, an arm, 85 per cent, a leg: what percentage, at least, must have lost all four?

SOLUTIONS

Lewis Carroll often posed mathematical questions or puzzles that he himself found difficult to answer or that he knew would perplex and divide fellow mathematicians. His questions can sometimes be a little open-ended and Carroll's solutions, many of which we provide here, are not always definitive or the only possible solution.

DOWN THE RABBIT-HOLE *p.13*

After falling Alice would oscillate back and forth between the point she entered and a point on the opposite side of the Earth. Because gravity acts towards the centre of the Earth, alternately accelerating and decelerating Alice, at the far side her velocity would be zero and she could simply hop out. Of course this doesn't take into account air resistance which would slow her journey through the hole and the Coriolis force caused by the Earth's rotation which would likely crush her into the walls. There is also the matter of the intense air pressure and temperature that would certainly do for poor Alice on her journey.

The average distance from the surface of the earth to its centre is 6,371 km (3,959 miles) so Alice is correct in her rough approximation.

DRINK ME *p.15*

Each tumbler starts and ends with exactly 50 spoonfuls of liquid. However much brandy ends up in the second tumbler, it must have been replaced with an equal amount of water.

A BOATING TRIP *p.17*

The first letter of each line spells out the name of Lewis Carroll's muse Alice Pleasance Liddell.

BUT A DREAM *p.19*

The first letter of each line, as well as the first three letters of the first line of each verse, spells Isa Bowman. Bowman (1874–1958) was a friend and actress who played Alice in the 1888 revival of the stage version of *Alice in Wonderland* at London's Globe Theatre.

HOW PUZZLING! *p.20*

Martin Gardener in *The Annotated Alice* suggests that Alice may never get to 20 because if you continue her nonsense progression: 4 x 5 is 12, 4 x 6 is 13, 4 x 7 is 14, and so on, you end with 4 x 12 is 19 because school multiplication tables typically end with 12.

Lewis Carroll may simply be showing how confused Alice is since leaving the normal world or how children, like the real Alice Liddell, sometimes had difficulty understanding numbers.

CATS AND RATS *p.24*

Assuming rat-killing rates are identical for each cat and constant throughout: 6 cats kill 6 rats in 6 minutes.
Therefore, 6 cats kill 1 rat in 1 minute,
6 cats kill 50 rats in 50 minutes,
and 12 cats kill 100 rats in 50 minutes.

Lewis Carroll, however, offers four different possible answers, showing that purely abstract solutions might not tell the whole story in the real world.

But when we come to trace the history of this sanguinary scene through all its horrid details, we find that at the end of 48 minutes 96 rats are dead and that there remain 4 live rats and 2 minutes to kill them in: the question is, can this be done?

Now there are at least four different ways in which the original feat of 6 cats killing 6 rats in 6 minutes, may be achieved. For the sake of clearness let us tabulate them:

A. All 6 cats are needed to kill a rat; and this they do in one minute, the other rats standing meekly by, waiting their turn.
B. 3 cats are needed to kill a rat, and they do it in 2 minutes.

C. 2 cats are needed, and they do it in 3 minutes.

D. Each cat kills a rat all by itself, and takes 6 minutes to do it.

In cases A and B it is clear that the 12 cats (who are assumed to come quite fresh from their 48 minutes of slaughter) can finish the affair in the required time; but, in case C, it can only be done by supposing that 2 cats could kill two-thirds of a rat in 2 minutes; and in case D, by supposing that a cat could kill one-third of a rat in 2 minutes. Neither supposition is warranted by the data; nor could the fractional rats (even if endowed with equal vitality) be fairly assigned to the different cats. For my part, if I were a cat in case D, and did not find my claws in good working order, I should certainly prefer to have my one-third-rat cut off from the tail end.

In cases C and D, then, it is clear that we must provide extra cat-power.

In case C less than 2 extra cats would be of no use. If 2 were supplied, and if they began killing their 4 rats at the beginning of the time, they would finish them in 12 minutes, and have 36 minutes to spare, during which they might weep, like Alexander, because there were not 12 more rats to kill. In case D, one extra cat would suffice; it would kill its 4 rats in 24 minutes, and have 24 minutes to spare, during which it could have killed another 4. But in neither case could any use be made of the last 2 minutes, except to half-kill rats – a barbarity we need not take into consideration.

To sum up our results. If the 6 cats kill the 6 rats by method A or B, the answer is "12"; if by method C, "14"; if by method D, "13."

This, then, is an instance of a solution made "indefinite" by the circumstances of the case.

A FOX, A GOOSE AND A BAG OF CORN *p.25*

One solution is the man takes the goose over first, leaves it there and returns for the corn, leaving it on the other side. He then returns with the goose, takes the fox to the other side, leaving it there with the corn, then returns for the goose.

WHERE DOES THE DAY BEGIN? *p.27*

In 1849 Lewis Carroll nor anyone else could answer this question. The issue was resolved in 1884 with the establishment of the International Date Line, an imaginary line on the Earth's surface which defines the boundary between one day and the next. Running from the North Pole to the South Pole through the Pacific Ocean, areas to the west of the Date Line are one calendar day ahead of areas to the east.

ANAGRAMS *p.29*

Wild agitator! Means well – William Ewart Gladstone
Flit on, cheering angel – Florence Nightingale

STOP THE CLOCKS *p.36*

These two puzzles appear as part of a discussion presented by Lewis Carroll, given below. The unnamed reader begins absolutely convinced that the answers are (1) the clock that is right twice a day is better, and (2) the clock that loses a minute every day is preferable. As you will see, Carroll then goes on to have far too much fun tying the unwitting reader in knots.

Which is the best, a clock that is right only once a year, or a clock that is right twice every day? "The latter," you reply, "unquestionably." Very good, reader, now attend.

I have two clocks: one doesn't go at all, and the other loses a minute a day: which would you prefer? "The losing one," you answer, "without a doubt." Now observe: the one which loses a minute a day has to lose twelve hours, or seven hundred and twenty minutes before it is right again, consequently it is only right once in two years, whereas the other is evidently right as often as the time it points to comes round, which happens twice a day. So you've contradicted yourself once. "Ah, but," you say, "what's the use of its being right twice a day, if I can't tell when the time comes?" Why, suppose the clock points to eight o'clock, don't you see that the clock is right at eight o'clock? Consequently when eight o'clock comes your clock is right. "Yes, I see that," you reply. Very good, then you've contradicted yourself twice: now get out of the difficulty as you can, and don't contradict yourself again if you can help it.

FOUR GENTLEMEN AND THEIR WIVES *p.50*

Suppose the four men are M1, M2, M3, M4 and their wives are, respectively, L1, L2, L3, L4. Here is one possible set of crossings:

M1 and L1 cross, M1 returns, M2 and L2 cross, M2 returns, M1 and M2 cross, M1 and L1 return, L1 and L3 cross, M2 returns, M1 and M2 cross, L3 returns, M3 and M4 cross, M3 returns, M3 and L3 cross, M4 returns, M4 and L4 cross.

MAGIC NUMBERS *p.51*

A. 2 x 142,857 = 285,714, 3 x 142,857 = 428,571, 4 x 142,857 = 571,428,
5 x 142,857 = 714,285, 6 x 142,857 – 857,142, 7 x 142,857 = 999,999
If you begin at 1 in each answer, the numbers are in the same order, whereas seven times the magic number is a row of 9's.

B. The number you get is 1089. For example, if you begin with 643, the reverse is 346. 643 – 346 = 297. Add 297 and its reverse 792 and you get 1089. If you try the same calculations with other numbers with decreasing digits the answer is always 1089.

THE MONKEY AND THE WEIGHT *p.52*

In a diary entry of 21 December 1893 Lewis Carroll writes that fellow mathematicians had come up with various solutions: his former tutor Bartholomew Price said the weight went *up* with increasing velocity, Clifton and Harcourt said the weight went up at the same rate as the monkey, while Sampson said it went *down*. In a letter to Bartholomew Price Carroll added the postscript: 'I own to an inclination to believe that the weight neither rises nor falls.' So, Carroll's belief was that as the monkey climbed up the rope, it and the weight would remain at the same level. The puzzle has continued to tease mathematicians, many of whom believe that the monkey and the weight would always remain opposite each other until both reached the pulley at the same time.

DOUBLETS *p.54–64*

PIG	**FOUR**	**WHEAT**	**EYE**	**TEARS**	**PITCH**	**HARE**	**PITY**
pit	foul	cheat	dye	sears	pinch	hark	pits
sit	fool	cheap	die	stars	winch	hack	pins
sat	foot	cheep	did	stare	wench	sack	fins
say	fort	creep	**LID**	stale	tench	sock	find
STY	fore	creed		stile	tenth	soak	fond
	fire	breed		**SMILE**	**TENTS**	**SOAP**	food
	FIVE	**BREAD**					**GOOD**

POOR	**OAT**	**APE**	**COMB**	**ARMY**	**BEANS**	**QUELL**	**BUY**
boor	rat	are	come	arms	beams	quill	bud
book	rot	ere	home	aims	seams	quilt	bid
rook	roe	err	hole	dims	shams	guilt	aid
rock	**RYE**	ear	hale	dams	shame	guile	aim
rick		mar	hall	dame	shale	guide	arm
RICH		**MAN**	hail	name	shall	glide	ark
			HAIR	nave	shell	glade	ask
				NAVY	**SHELF**	grade	**ASS**
						grave	
						brave	
						BRAVO	

MINE	**KETTLE**	**OIL**	**JOHN**	**SHAVE**	**BROWN**	**ORE**	**DOOR**
mint	settle	nil	join	share	brawn	are	poor
mist	settee	nip	loin	stare	brain	arm	pour
most	setter	nap	loon	stars	braid	aim	pout
moat	better	gap	look	sears	brand	him	gout
coat	betted	**GAS**	lock	bears	bland	hem	glut
COAL	belted		lack	**BEARD**	blank	**GEM**	**GLUE**
	bolted		**JACK**		**BLACK**		
	bolter						
	bolder						
	HOLDER						

ONE	**SORRY**	**MILLER**	**ODE**	**TOOTH**	**OIL**	**FEAR**	**IDEA**
owe	worry	milled	odd	booth	ail	hear	ides
ewe	wordy	misled	add	boots	air	head	odes
eye	words	missed	aid	blots	sir	held	odds
rye	wards	massed	did	blows	six	hold	adds
roe	warps	masked	din	blown	sex	hole	aids
rob	harps	marked	dun	brown	**SEA**	**HOPE**	airs
JOB	harpy	**MARKET**	**SUN**	drown			firs
	HAPPY			**DRAWN**			fire
							fare
							face
							FACT

OWL	**ETHEL**	**DEBTS**	**ELMS**	**BEAVER**	**GLAND**	**JOE**	**TILES**
oil	ether	dents	alms	braver	bland	doe	tills
ail	other	bents	aims	braves	blank	die	tells
aim	otter	beats	dims	braces	clank	did	sells
rim	outer	seats	dies	traces	clans	aid	seals
ram	muter	sears	died	tracts	clams	and	sears
JAM	mutes	spars	deed	traits	crams	**ANN**	stars
	mites	spare	weed	trains	trams		stare
	mines	spire	**WEEP**	brains	teams		state
	miner	spine		braids	**TEARS**		**SLATE**
	miser	swine		brands			
	WISER	swing		**BRANDY**			
		OWING					

HOAX	**THUR**	**STALK**	**JACK**	**DINNER**	**OARS**	**LOSS**	**VEAL**
coax	tour	stale	sack	sinner	bars	lass	real
coal	sour	stare	sick	singer	bass	laws	reel
cool	soar	scare	silk	linger	boss	lawn	reef
FOOL	star	score	sill	longer	boas	lain	**BEEF**
	stay	scorn	**JILL**	conger	**BOAT**	**GAIN**	
	SDAY	**ACORN**		confer			
				coffer			
				COFFEE			

NOUN	**SHIP**	**PLANT**	**MONK**	**WASH**	**WITH**	**UNIT**	**COMET**
noon	slip	plans	mock	wish	wits	knit	comes
moon	slap	plats	cock	wise	bits	knot	domes
morn	soap	peats	cork	wile	bias	knob	dames
more	soak	beats	core	will	boas	snob	dazes
mere	sock	**BEANS**	come	**WELL**	boar	snub	gazes
here	**DOCK**		**ROME**		soar	snug	**GAZER**
herb					**SOAP**	slug	
VERB						slur	
						sour	
						FOUR	

ADA	**PICT**	**HORSE**	**AYE**	**CRY**	**OPEN**	**SMILES**	**AIR**
add	pint	house	bye	coy	oven	smiled	fir
aid	pins	rouse	bee	cot	even	soiled	far
bid	pies	route	bet	cut	eves	coiled	fay
bad	dies	routs	yet	**OUT**	eyes	cooled	**FLY**
ban	dyes	bouts	**YES**		dyes	cooked	
FAN	eyes	boats			does	choked	
	ewes	brats			dots	**CHOKER**	
	owes	brass			dote		
	ores	**GRASS**			date		
	URES				**GATE**		

CURL	**BOWLER**	**LIE**	**FEBR**	**NAILS**	**TIE**	**STUDY**	**HAIL**
cull	bowled	lit	fear	hails	die	studs	sail
call	cowled	lot	pear	hairs	dim	stuns	said
hall	cooled	**NOT**	peat	heirs	aim	stunt	slid
hail	cooked		pert	hears	**ARM**	stint	sled
HAIR	looked		part	heard		saint	slew
	locked		wart	beard		**FAINT**	slow
	licked		wary	**BOARD**			**SNOW**
	wicked		**UARY**				
	WICKET						

WOE	**HUNT**	**BUTTER**	**CRAB**	**CORN**	**SHUT**	**BEAT**	**TEACH**
doe	punt	better	crag	cork	shot	boat	tench
die	pent	beater	brag	cook	soot	boas	tenth
did	sent	beaver	brat	coop	boot	**BOYS**	tents
aid	seat	weaver	**BOAT**	crop	boor		tints
and	sear	weaves		crow	**DOOR**		tilts
END	star	leaves		**GROW**			tills
	STAG	**LOAVES**					gills
							GIRLS

THE WHITE RABBIT *p.65*

The '9' Trick – When you reverse the digits of a number and then subtract it from the original number, the sum of the digits of the result is always a multiple of 9. So, if a person removes a digit from the answer, you can work out how much needs to be added to make a sum divisible by 9. For example, 8164 – 4618 = 3546, and if they remove the number 4, they are left with 3+5+6, which totals 14. To make a sum divisible by 9, you need to add 4 to make 18, so you know the digit that was removed was 4.

The Addition Sum – When the person gives you the first number you add it to 9999 + 9999 (so 2563 + 9999 + 9999 = 22,561). Then whichever number the person chooses, you subtract it from 9999. So 9999 – 2146 = 7853 and 9999 – 6732 = 3267. Adding the five numbers 2563, 2146, 7853, 6732 and 3267 = 22,561. (The only caveat with this method is if the person chooses a second or third four-digit number which starts with 9, you are forced to come up with a three-digit number or if they pick 9999, you have to pick 0!)

Counting Alternately – After the person had chosen a number you subtract it from 11 and then choose your number, so if the person chooses 5, you add 6, then if they add 4, you add 7 and so on. This strategy is a guaranteed win for the second player, but if you are the first player, there is nothing you can do – except hope that your opponent makes an error.

MIRROR IMAGE *p.71*

The phrases are: (A) 'Curiouser and curiouser!' (B) 'When *I* use a word,' Humpty Dumpty said in rather a scornful tone, 'it means just what I choose it to mean – neither more nor less.' (C) 'Off with his head!' (D) 'Why, sometimes I've believed as many as six impossible things before breakfast.'

A SQUARE WINDOW *p.74*

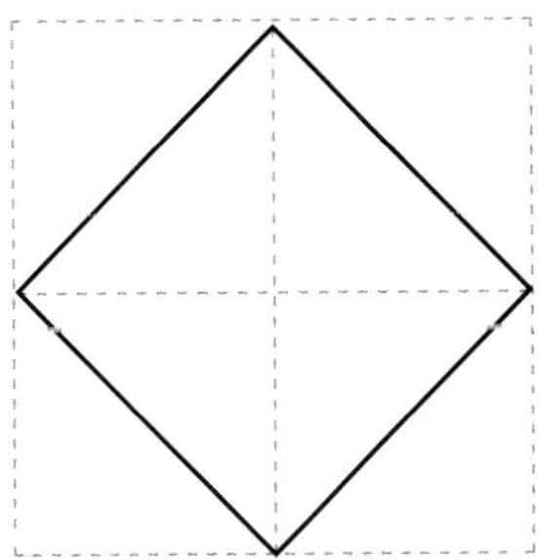

The original square can be split into 8 congruent (identical) triangles, 4 of which make up the new window; so the area of the new window (and thus the amount of light permitted) is halved.

THREE SQUARES *p.77*

This shows how you could draw the squares – there are other possible solutions.

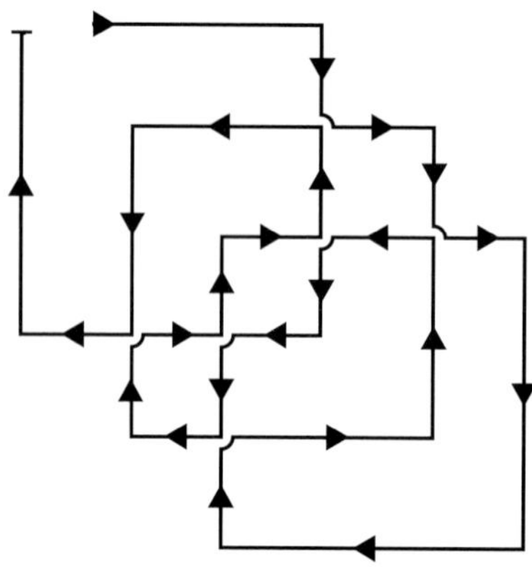

HOW TO BALANCE AN EGG *p.79*

Legend has it that the explorer Christopher Columbus stood an egg on its tip by tapping an egg on a table to flatten its tip. Another way to do it is to pour a small mound of salt on a table, set the egg upright on to it and then carefully remove the excess grains with a fine brush or by gently blowing until it looks as if the egg is unsupported.

DAYS OF THE WEEK *p.80*

A. Friday B. Friday C. Saturday D. Wednesday E. Friday

MAZE *p.84*

Here is one solution.

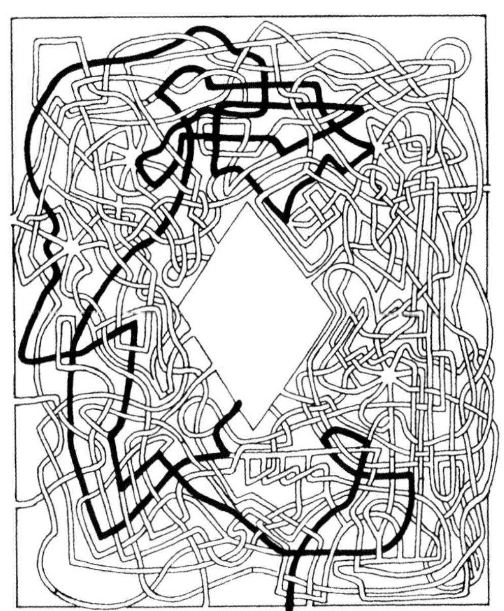

RUNNING RACES *p.87*

A should have a 44-yard start and C should have a 40-yard handicap.

VERSE RIDDLES *p.89*

1. Ten apples would appear, as hidden in the second line 'And dreaming of-ten, dear.'
2. Sawdust would diminish the weight, meaning each piece would weigh just short of a quarter of a pound (or just less than 4 ounces).

A BOX RIDDLE *p.93*

This is the solution that appeared in *Aunt Judy's Magazine* in 1870 attributed to 'Eadgyth' who was probably a staff member of the magazine.

As curly-wigg'd Jemmy was sleeping in bed
His brother John gave him a blow on the head;
James opened his eyelids, and spying his brother,
Doubled his fist, and gave him another.
This kind of box then is not so rare;
The lids are the eyelids, the locks are the hair;
And as every schoolboy can tell to his cost,
The key to the tangles is constantly lost.

(The box, therefore, is a boxing punch.)

A CAPTIVE QUEEN *p.94*

Here is one possible solution. The weight is sent down, the son goes down and the weight comes up. The weight is sent down again, the daughter goes down, and the son and the weight come up together. The weight is sent down, the son goes down, and the weight come up. The queen and the weight go down, and the son and daughter come up. The son goes down and the weight comes up. The weight is sent down, the daughter goes down, and the son and the weight come up. The weight is sent down, the son goes down, and the weight goes up.

SITTING IN A CIRCLE *p.105*

A. There were 7 men. B. 2 shillings.

Here is one way to solve this complex problem. Suppose there are n men. When the transfer of shillings is no longer possible, the second last man will have 0 shillings, the third last 1 shilling, the fourth last 2 shillings, and so on, with the first man having n - 2 shillings, and the last man having all the remaining money.

For example, if there are 4 men and they start with 6 shillings, 5 shillings, 4 shillings and 3 shillings. After 15 transfers they will have 2 shillings, 1 shilling, 0 shillings and 15 shillings. At this point, the last man is expected to transfer 16 shillings to the first man, but they cannot, so the process stops.

Keep working on this and it becomes clear that the only way for someone to have exactly 4 times their neighbour, is for the last person to have exactly 4 times as much as the first person. By doing this you arrive at the unique solution that there were 7 men starting with the following totals: 8 shillings, 7 shillings, 6 shillings, 5 shillings, 4 shillings, 3 shillings and 2 shillings (the poorest man).

After 20 transfers, they will have: 5 shillings, 4 shillings, 3 shillings, 2 shillings, 1 shilling, 0 shillings and 20 shillings. At this point they have to stop, with the last person (20 shillings) having 4 times as much as the first person (5 shillings).

WHAT'S IN THE BAG? *p.106*

Here is Lewis Carroll's solution from *Pillow-Problems.*

> The 'a priori' chances of possible states of first bag are 'W, ½; B, ½.
> Hence chances, after putting W in, are "W W, ½; WB, ½.
> The chances, which these give to the 'observed event' are 1, ½.
> Hence chances of possible states 'W, B', after the event, are proportional to 1, ½; i.e. to 2, 1; i.e. their actual values are ⅔, ⅓.
> Now, in first course, chance of drawing W is ½•⅔+½•⅓; i.e. ½.
> And, in second course, chances of possible states "WWBB, WBBB' are ⅔, ⅓: hence chance of drawing W is ⅔•½ + ⅓•¼; i.e 5⁄12
> Hence *first* course gives best chance.

CAT FEEDING *p.109*

Puss wouldn't eat from the third sister because she gave 'her ring' ('herring').

THE KING AND HIS WISE MEN *p.110*

He kept sixteen wise men.

DOUBLETS *p.113–122*

GRIND	**WIND**	**MAR**	**OWL**
grins	wend	mad	oil
grips	weed	bad	nil
trips	feed	bed	nib
traps	fled	bee	bib
trams	flew	**BLE**	bob
drams	flow		**BOY**
drags	**BLOW**		
DRUGS			

NORTH	**BIPED**	**FOUR**	**EAG**	**ALOE**	**DREAM**	**CAS**	**SEEK**
forth	wiped	sour	lag	sloe	cream	can	reek
forts	wipes	soar	leg	slop	creak	tan	reed
ports	wiles	sear	**LES**	slip	croak	tin	rend
pouts	wales	seer		slid	crack	tie	rind
bouts	**WALKS**	seen		said	clack	**TLE**	**FIND**
boots		**TEEN**		sand	slack		
booth				sank	stack		
sooth				**BANK**	stark		
SOUTH					**STARS**		

CALF	**SOLU**	**ENTER**	**MIX**	**PULL**	**WRITE**	**LOVER**	**SPIN**
call	sold	eater	six	poll	writs	loves	shin
tall	told	water	sex	pool	waits	coves	chin
tell	toad	waver	sea	poor	warts	cores	**COIN**
teal	load	waves	**TEA**	pour	parts	corps	
VEAL	loan	raves		sour	ports	carps	
	loon	raven		slur	poets	harps	
	lion	**HAVEN**		slug	**POEMS**	harpy	
	TION			**PLUG**		**HAPPY**	

WARM	**CARRY**	**VIEW**	**SPELL**	**CINDER**	**GOLD**	**CAST**	**STAND**
wars	curry	vies	spill	tinder	bold	last	staid
tars	curly	dies	spilt	tender	bond	lost	stain
taps	curls	dims	stilt	tended	band	loss	slain
tops	culls	aims	stint	bended	bane	**LOTS**	plain
TOES	cults	ails	saint	beaded	lane		plait
	colts	**OILS**	paint	bladed	**LACE**		plant
	coots		pains	blamed			slant
	boots		wains	blames			slang
	BOOTY		warns	**FLAMES**			sling
			wards				sting
			WORDS				stint
							stilt
							STILL

KISS	**SELL**	**TRIP**	**PULL**	**FOR**	**CROSS**	**ASK**	**ELMS**
miss	seal	grip	poll	fir	crops	ark	alms
mass	seas	grin	pool	air	coops	arm	aims
bass	sees	gain	poop	ail	corps	aim	dims
base	bees	rain	prop	all	cores	him	dins
babe	byes	**RAIL**	prow	ill	coves	ham	dint
BABY	eyes		grow	ilk	cover	hay	hint
	eves		**GROG**	ink	rover	**WAY**	hilt
	even			**INN**	**RIVER**		**HILL**
	oven						
	OXEN						

CRABS	**CHECK**	**GREEKS**	**WHY**	**WREN**	**COURT**	**BREAK**	**FRY**
crass	chick	creeks	way	ween	count	creak	try
cross	thick	cheeks	bay	been	fount	creek	toy
crops	trick	checks	bad	beet	found	cheek	toe
coops	prick	chicks	bid	best	wound	check	doe
coots	price	chinks	aid	**NEST**	would	chick	dye
clots	prise	chines	add		**WORLD**	chink	aye
cloth	poise	chimes	**ADO**			**CHINA**	**APE**
SLOTH	**NOISE**	crimes					
		CRIMEA					

SHUT	**GAS**	**WEAR**	**BRING**	**DUST**	**CLASP**	**DAY**	**BEER**
shot	was	hear	brink	must	class	dam	beet
shod	war	heap	blink	most	clans	dim	bent
shed	ear	hemp	blank	moot	clank	aim	went
seed	err	hems	plank	root	clack	arm	wend
sees	ere	**GEMS**	plane	**ROOM**	clock	are	wind
bees	**EVE**		place		**CLOAK**	ace	**WINE**
byes			**PEACE**			**ICE**	
EYES							

OPEN	**ASP**	**HELP**	**HONEY**	**WHY**	**ROME**	**RUBY**	**RUSKS**
oven	ask	held	hones	way	role	rubs	busks
even	ark	heed	holes	war	roll	cubs	basks
eves	arm	seed	boles	ear	doll	cube	bases
eyes	aim	sped	bolts	**ERR**	dull	cure	bakes
byes	him	aped	boots		**BULL**	core	**BAKED**
bees	ham	**AGED**	booth			**CORN**	
fees	**HAY**		**BROTH**				
feel							
fell							
CELL							

BULL	**YELL**	**CRY**	**KEEP**	**DISC**	**AWL**	**ROAST**	**ANT**
full	dell	coy	keen	disk	ail	boast	and
furl	dull	boy	been	risk	aid	beast	aid
furs	duel	bey	bees	rise	bid	least	bid
firs	dues	bee	bets	ride	bad	leapt	bib
FIGS	dies	bye	bats	rids	wad	leaps	bob
	dims	**AYE**	oats	aids	**WAX**	leaks	**BOX**
	aims		**OATH**	adds		beaks	
	arms			odds		becks	
	arks			**ORDS**		decks	
	irks					**DUCKS**	
	iris						
	IBIS						

CONE	CURDS	REST	SHOES	TIGER	COSTS	ONE	BLUE
bone	cords	lest	shops	tiler	posts	owe	glue
bond	corns	lost	chops	tiles	pests	ewe	glut
bend	coins	loft	drops	tides	tests	eye	gout
send	chins	soft	cross	rides	tents	dye	pout
seed	chink	**SOFA**	cress	rises	tenth	doe	port
sped	chick		crest	**ROSES**	tench	toe	part
aped	check		**CRUST**		teach	too	pant
APEX	cheek				peach	**TWO**	pint
	creek				peace		**PINK**
	creak				**PENCE**		
	CREAM						

MISSING UNIT *p.123*

The extra unit comes from an inaccurate presentation of the rectangle. If one was to dissect the square and rearrange the pieces, this is what it would actually look like.

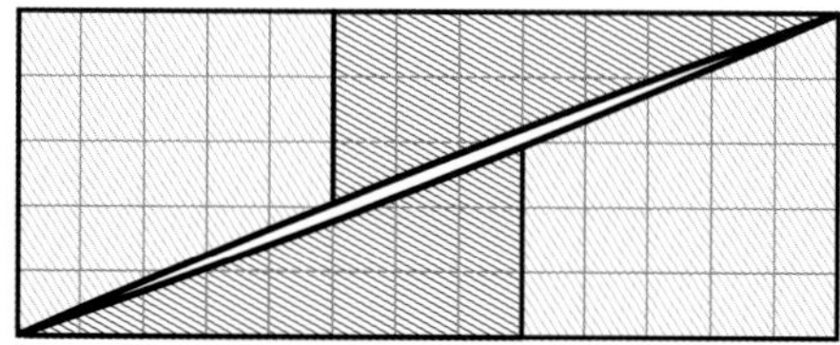

The slopes of the diagonal edges are close, but don't quite match up perfectly. This leaves a thin gap in the middle of the rectangle, of an area exactly 1 unit.

HIDDEN NAME *p.124*

The initials of Edith Rix are given in the second letter of each line.

DOUBLE ACROSTIC *p.126*

The initial letters of the first lines spell Gertrude Chataway, and the first words of each stanza also spell the name.

THE FISH RIDDLE *p.128*

The fish-dish is an oyster.

REBUS LETTER *p.130*

The Chestnuts *

My dear Ina

Though I don't give birthday *presents*, still I may write a birthday letter. I came to your door to wish you many happy returns for the day, but the cat met me, and took me for a mouse, and hunted me up and down till I could hardly stand. However *somehow* I got into the house, and there a mouse met me, and took me for a cat, and pelted me with fire-irons, pots and pans and wine-bottles. Of course I ran into the street again, and a horse met me and took me for a cart, and dragged me all the way to the Guildhall **, but the worst of all was when a cart met me and took me for a horse. I was harnessed to it, and had to draw it miles and miles, all the way to Merrow. So you see I couldn't get to the room where you were.

However I was glad to hear you were at work learning the multiplication tables for a birthday treat.

I had just time to look into the kitchen, and saw your birthday feast getting ready, a nice bowl of crusts, bones, pills, cotton-bobbins, and rhubarb and magnesia. "Now," I thought, "she will be happy!" and with a smile I went on my way.

Your aff[ectiona]te friend
CLD

* The Chestnuts was the home of Lewis Carroll's sisters in Guildford.
** The picture represents Guildhall, a landmark in the centre of Guildford, which would have been familiar to the letter's recipient Georgina Watson.

THE HUNTING OF THE SNARK *p.134*

The answer is three. The answer will always be the original number because the third verse reverses the calculations in the second verse.

ALPHABET CIPHER *p.136*

The extract decoded is as follows:
She stretched hereself up on tiptoe, and peeped over the edge of the mushroom, and her eyes immediately met those of a large blue caterpillar, that was sitting on the top, with its arms folded, quietly smoking a long hookah, and taking not the smallest notice of her or of anything else.

TWIDDLE YOUR EYES *p.140*

The sailor's name was Yvan. The lawyer's name Rab spelt backwards is bar, the soldier's name Ymra spelt backwards is army, and the sailor's name Yvan spelt backwards is navy!

A TANGLED TALE *p.143–157*

Here are the problems, answers and solutions provided by Lewis Carroll in *A Tangled Tale.*

KNOT I 'EXCELSIOR'

Problem—"Two travellers spend from 3 o' clock till 9 in walking along a level road, up a hill, and home again: their pace on the level being 4 miles an hour, up hill 3, and down hill 6. Find distance walked: also (within half an hour) time of reaching top of hill."

Answer—"24 miles: half-past 6."
Solution—A level mile takes ¼ of an hour, up hill ⅓, down hill ⅙. Hence to go and return over the same mile, whether on the level or on the hill-side, takes ½ an hour. Hence in 6 hours they went 12 miles out and 12 back. If the 12 miles out had been nearly all level, they would have taken a little over 3 hours; if nearly all up hill, a little under 4. Hence 3 ½ hours must be within ½ an hour of the time taken in reaching the peak; thus, as they started at 3, they got there within ½ an hour of ½ past 6.

KNOT II 'ELIGIBLE APARTMENTS'

1. THE DINNER PARTY.

Problem—"The Governor of Kgovjni wants to give a very small dinner party, and invites his father's brother-in-law, his brother's father-in-law, his father-in-law's brother, and his brother-in-law's father. Find the number of guests."
Answer—"One."

2. THE LODGINGS.

Problem—"A Square has 20 doors on each side, which contains 21 equal parts. They are numbered all round, beginning at one corner. From which of the four, Nos. 9, 25, 52, 73, is the sum of the distances, to the other three, least?"
Answer —"From No. 9."

Problem—(1) "Two travellers, starting at the same time, went opposite ways round a circular railway. Trains start each way every 15 minutes, the easterly ones going round in 3 hours, the westerly in 2. How many trains did each meet on the way, not counting trains met at the terminus itself?" (2) "They went round, as before, each traveller counting as 'one' the train containing the other traveller. How many did each meet?"
Answers—(1) 19. (2) The easterly traveller met 12; the other 8.

The trains one way took 180 minutes, the other way 120. Let us take the L. C. M., 360, and divide the railway into 360 units. Then one set of trains went at the rate of 2 units a minute and at intervals of 30 units; the other at the rate of 3 units a minute and at intervals of 45 units. An easterly train starting has 45 units between it and the first train it will meet: it does 2-5ths of this while the other does 3-5ths, and thus meets it at the end of 18 units, and so all the way round. A westerly train starting has 30 units between it and the first train it will meet: it does 3-5ths of this while the other does 2-5ths, and thus meets it at the end of 18 units, and so all the way round. Hence if the railway be divided, by 19 posts, into 20 parts, each containing 18 units, trains meet at every post, and, in (1), each traveller passes 19 posts in going round, and so meets 19 trains. But, in (2), the easterly traveller only begins to count after traversing 2-5ths of the journey, *i.e.*, on reaching the 8th post, and so counts 12 posts: similarly the other counts 8. They meet at the end of 2-5ths of 3 hours, or 3-5ths of 2 hours, *i.e.*, 72 minutes.

1. In 6¼ minutes.
2. *Answer* —Ten. *Solution*—For each 100 men, 70 + 75 + 80 + 85= 310 parts have been lost, so only 400 - 310 = 90 parts remain. Even if the 90 parts were distributed among as many men as possible, that is 1 to each of 90 men, there would still be 10 men to have lost all four.

ACKNOWLEDGEMENTS

The extracts on pages 16 and 75 are reproduced courtesy of The Trustees of the C L Dodgson Estate. Thank you also to Caroline Luke and Emily Talbot.

Many thanks to mathematical consultant Daniel Griller for his guidance and contributions. Thanks also to Mark and Catherine Richards for their help in identifying source material, Mark Frary for his contribution to the rabbit-hole entry and Esther Marriott for her work on the cipher extract. Many thanks to designer Clare Sivell and Lindsay Nash, Lydia Ramah, Kelly Collins and Ingrid Connell at Macmillan.

BIBLIOGRAPHY AND SOURCES

BOOKS

Carroll, Lewis, *Alice's Adventures in Wonderland* (Macmillan, 2014)

Carroll, Lewis, *Doublets A Word-puzzle,* (Macmillan and Co, 1879)

Carroll, Lewis, *The Hunting of the Snark* (Macmillan, 1993)

Carroll, Lewis, *The Mathematical Recreations of Lewis Carroll* (Dover Publications, 2003)

Carroll, Lewis, *Phantasmagoria* (Macmillan and Co, 1869)

Carroll, Lewis, *Sylvie and Bruno* (Macmillan and Co, 1889)

Carroll, Lewis, *Sylvie and Bruno Concluded* (Macmillan and Co, 1893)

Carroll, Lewis, *A Tangled Tale* (Macmillan and Co, 1885)

Carroll, Lewis, *Through the Looking-Glass and What Alice Found There* (Macmillan, 2021)

Cohen, Morten N., ed, *The Letters of Lewis Carroll* (OUP, 1979)

Cohen, Morten Cohen, *Lewis Carroll, Interviews and Reflections* (Macmillan Press, 1989)

Collingwood, Stuart Dodgson, ed, *The Lewis Carroll Picture Book* (Fisher Unwin, 1899)

Collingwood, Stuart Dodgson, ed, *The Life and Letters of Lewis Carroll*, (Fisher Unwin, 1898)

Dodgson, Charles L., *Pillow-Problems Thought Out During Wakeful Hours*, Second Edition, (Macmillan and Company Ltd, 1885)

Fisher, John, ed, *The Magic of Lewis Carroll* (Penguin Books, 1975)

Gardner, Martin, ed, *The Annotated Alice* (Penguin Books, 2001)

Gardner, Martin, ed, *The Annotated Snark* (Penguin Books, 1974)

Green, Roger Lancelyn, ed, *The Diaries of Lewis Carroll Volume II* (Cassell, 1953)

Hatch, Evelyn M., ed, *A Selection of the Letters of Lewis Carroll to his Child-Friends*, (Macmillan and Co, 1933)

Hudson, Derek, *Lewis Carroll* (Constable, 1954)

Loyd, Sam, *Sam Loyd's Cyclopedia of 5000 Puzzles, Tricks and Conundrums with Answers* (The Lamb Publishing Company, 1914)

Morgan, Christopher, *The Pamphlets of Lewis Carroll, Volume 5 Games, Puzzles and Related Pieces*, (The Lewis Carroll Society of North America, University Press of Virginia, 2015)

Wakeling, Edward, ed, *Lewis Carroll's Diaries: The Private Journals of Charles Lutwidge Dodgson Volumes 1–10* (The Lewis Carroll Society, 1993-2007)

Wakeling, Edward, ed, *Lewis Carroll's Games and Puzzles* (Dover Publications, 1992)

Wakeling, Edward, ed, *Rediscovered Lewis Carroll Puzzles* (Dover Publications, 1995)

Wilson, Robin, *Lewis Carroll in Numberland* (Penguin Books, 2008)

PAMPHLETS AND ARTICLES

Carroll, Lewis, Castle Croquêt (1866) (*Aunt Judy's Magazine*, 1867)

Carroll, Lewis, Puzzles from Wonderland (*Aunt Judy's Magazine*, December 1870)

Carroll, Lewis, Lanrick (16 January 1879)

Carroll, Lewis, Mischmasch (*Court Circular*, 2 December 1886)

Carroll, Lewis, 'To Find the Day of the Week for any Given Date', *Nature* 35, 517, 31 March 1887.

The Doublets Columns, *Vanity Fair*, 29 March 1879–9 April 1881 (doublets written either by Lewis Carroll or Editors of *Vanity Fair*)

AFTERWORD

When is a Riddle not a Riddle?

When, of course, it doesn't have a solution. Which is why in this book we give you a final puzzling riddle *after* you've checked out the 'solutions' to all the other riddles and puzzles.

If you haven't guessed – and many of you will have been wondering when we would get around to it – it is the riddle posed by the Hatter at the Mad Tea-Party.

> 'You should learn not to make personal remarks,' Alice said with some severity; 'it's very rude.'
>
> The Hatter opened his eyes very wide on hearing this; but all he *said* was, 'Why is a raven like a writing-desk?'
>
> 'Come, we shall have some fun now!' thought Alice. 'I'm glad they've begun asking riddles – I believe I can guess that,' she added aloud.

But Alice's hopefulness is, sadly, misplaced since, a little later in this unsatisfying tea-party, the Hatter returns to his question:

> 'Have you guessed the riddle yet?' the Hatter said, turning to Alice again.
>
> 'No, I give it up,' Alice replied: 'what's the answer?'
>
> 'I haven't the slightest idea,' said the Hatter.
>
> 'Nor I,' said the March Hare.
>
> Alice sighed wearily. 'I think you might do something better with the time,' she said, 'than waste it in asking riddles that have no answers.'

Alice's response causes the Hatter to reflect, at length, about the nature (and 'person') of Time and the riddle is momentarily forgotten. But readers of *Alice's Adventures* did not forget and, indeed, a great many approached the author with a request for a solution.

This Carroll finally provided in a new preface to the 1896 edition of *Wonderland*:

> Enquiries have been so often addressed to me, as to whether any answer to the Hatter's Riddle can be imagined, that I may as well put on record here what seems to me to be a fairly appropriate answer, viz: 'Because it can produce a few notes, tho they are very flat; and it is never put with the wrong end in front!' This, however, is merely an afterthought; the Riddle, as originally invented, had no answer at all.

The 'very flat notes' are a good start, but the part about never being put the wrong end in front seems curiously unsatisfactory and remained so until 1976 when Carroll scholar Denis Crutch discovered that when that answer was first published the word 'never' was given as 'nevar' (or 'raven' put with the wrong end in front!) and that, seemingly, this apparent spelling error had then been 'corrected' (perhaps by a diligent proof-reader) in all subsequent editions.

In any event, the reading public has remained obsessed with this unanswered riddle and many alternative solutions have been suggested. The American puzzle genius Sam Loyd offered several possible ripostes such as: 'Because the notes for which they are noted are not noted for being musical notes'; or 'Because bills and tales are among their characteristics' and, perhaps most apt, 'Because Poe wrote on both', a reference to writer Edgar Allen Poe who penned the well-known poem 'The Raven'.

Across 160 years there has been no shortage of other contenders: 'Because one has flapped fits and the other fitting flaps'; 'Because it bodes ill for owed bills'; and 'Because both have quills dipped in ink.'

'Why is a raven like a writing-desk?' is, without doubt, Lewis Carroll's most celebrated brainteaser, but would it still have been as famous if the Hatter had given Alice an answer to his riddle? Obviously, that would depend on the cleverness or funniness of the answer. But the fact that the character in the story (and the writer who created him) asked a question which, at the time, had no answer is what renders it *truly* famous and for two reasons.

Firstly, it goes to the very heart of what makes nonsense so intriguing and enticing (or, conversely, annoying and frustrating), a game where there are no rules or a requirement to make sense! What kind of an anarchy would result if we all asked questions that have no answers?

Secondly, and possibly most importantly, puzzles without solutions and riddles without answers, are a reminder that – however uneasy they might make us feel – life and the world around us teems with enigmas, paradoxes and *non sequiturs* and one of the most comfortable ways – perhaps the *only* comfortable way – of approaching them is in a spirit of light-hearted playfulness.

Now, in that very spirit, you can happily set about inventing an infinite number of possible answers to the question of why a raven is like a writing-desk, confident of never being wrong! Or, better still, if you've been inspired by this book, follow Lewis Carroll's example and try your hand at devising and sharing head-scratching, brain-wracking puzzles of your own!

– BRIAN SIBLEY

BRIAN SIBLEY is a writer and dramatist with a passionate interest in children's literature and fantasy fiction on which he has extensively written, lectured and broadcast. He is also a long-standing member of The Lewis Carroll Society in Great Britain, having served as Secretary and President and is currently the Society's Chair. You can find out more about The Lewis Carroll Society here: www.lewiscarrollsociety.org.uk